Tools of Intention
Strategies that Inspire Change

Stephen R. Lankton

Published by

Stephen R. Lankton, MSW, DAHB, LLC

P.O. Box 9489, Phoenix, Arizona 85068, USA

www. lankton.com

© 2008 by Stephen R. Lankton

All rights reserved.

No part of this publication may be reproduced, stored in a retrieval system, transmitted or utilized in any form by any means, electronic, mechanical, photocopying or recording or otherwise, without permission in writing from the publishers.

Manufactured in the United Sates of America.

Acknowledgments

I want to thank the hundreds of clients and thousands of trainees who have allowed me to work with and teach them over the past three decades. Their questions, feedback, goals, and successes have shaped my work and ideas immeasurably. The ideas and steps in this book are a co-creation of working together with my clients and trainees.

Most of all I want to thank Milton H. Erickson, M.D., of Phoenix, Arizona. He was an unshakable example of the spirit behind the material in this book –he lived it as a model for others.

For more information about the life of Milton Erickson refer to: Short, D., Erickson, B. A., & Erickson-Klein, R. (2005). *Hope and Resiliency: Understanding the Psychotherapeutic Strategies of Milton H. Erickson, MD*. Crown House Publishing

Table of Contents

1. Inspiration 1
2. Tools to Express Intention 3
3. Chunking Logic and "Magic Markers" 7
4. Self-Hypnosis 19
5. Appreciation Lists 31
6. Vivid Symbolic Imagery... 37
7. Heart Joy 45
8. Self-Image Thinking 51
9. Future Creating Emanated Images 67
10. Self-Reparenting and Self-Nurturing Spirals 73
11. Bioenergy and Chakra Balancing 83
12. Responsibility and Empowerment 89

1. Inspiration

Breathing - it is the cycle of inhalation or inspiration and exhalation or expiration. When it leaves a person permanently we say the person has expired, that their spirit has left. When we are filled from within by vital energy we are said to be inspired and our spirit is enriched.

We are also inspired by our intention. Yet, little has been written about *using* intention to achieve what we want in our lives. Intention is something that comes from within. It can fill us and inform us as it shapes and drives our spirit.

The tools in this book promote positive *experiencing* by using imagination and thinking. They are not just positive *thinking*. The popular book and DVD about the "secret" is not really *the* secret – it is mindful visualization. Visualizations alone will not magically "draw" great things to people. Much more than just positive thinking and visualizing needs to occur to give you control of your destiny. This book is about the *real* steps necessary to effectively use your intention to design and change your life.

The tool described in chapter six - Vivid Symbolic Imagery - does in fact make use of visualization, but for producing and strengthening feelings and experiences that put your unconscious mind in motion to achieve your goals. The resulting experiences will transform your self-image and be reflected in your smile, your gait, your selection of words, and also, in time, your entire interpersonal presentation. When you look and act different to others, your world *will* change! You will communicate, in subtle and obvious ways, your path and direction. We know that 93% of all communication is non-verbal. So, when you interact with others while having the experiences you need to be congruent with your intention you will appear inspired. You will literally stand behind your words. This will be revealed by both your verbal as well as your non-verbal communication. The result will be quite powerful.

People who hear and see you will sense your intention. If they are to be helpers and allies they will sense that you are a good fit and they will be attracted. You will receive opportunities and trust because you will appear and be capable. To those who are on a different path – those who don't mean business, those who are playing games - you will not be attractive. They will see that you are solid and not what they are looking for. They will go elsewhere to play their games. The consequences that follow these subtle communication changes will result in the original promise of the, so called, secret. But not by magic. Rather, by interpersonal selection.

The expression of intention by means of these tools will attract what you want in feelings, attitudes, and even measurable, interpersonal goals – and if there is a metaphysical component then so much the better. But desired and needed experience, attitude, and behavior is the goal. Each tool is a fundamentally different method to get the experiences you need in the context in which you need them – to inspire yourself. *That* is what constitutes health and happiness.

2. Tools To Express Intention

I am sometimes shocked, surprised, saddened, and appalled at how little individuals of any age know how to use their mind and experiences for their own benefit. As a young boy I had a curiosity that was apparently more active than most of the people around me. I remember one time when I became introspective and tried to do some thinking about my thinking. That's not a typographical error, I actually drew a map or schema that to the best of my ability depicted the thinking I had done about the manner in which I used pictures and words in order to think. As I recall, the map displayed larger and smaller overlapping rectangles connected here and there by straight lines. The rectangles represented visual memories or anticipations often embedded within one another while the straight lines represented self-talk, words, and labels that I used to connect them. I was surprised that no one else in my family had ever had such an introspection. I remember that both of my parents and my sister responded with, "I don't know" when I asked them to describe how they think. I soon forgot about the incident.

It would be years later before I would discover the science of psychology. And a few years after that before I would discover the philosophical branch of epistemology. Here too, however, I was quite surprised at the typically distant and hands-off understanding provided by the experts in those fields. Of course, sciences that have to be constructed by means of a reductionistic and materialistic approach to nature are only going to be able to reach so far.

Introspection as a tool for understanding the mind is more popular in Hindu, especially, and Buddhist cultures. But the object of the introspection done by their yogis and monks has primarily been concerned with spiritual ascension. And while there is definitive value in such matters, they still leave a large gap in understanding how to use thinking and experiencing for those of us who aren't planning to ascend anytime soon.

Having been a psychotherapist for 35 years, and a student of psychotherapy for even longer, I studied and worked with some of the best luminaries in psychology, psychotherapy, and psychiatry that ever lived and practiced. Over the years I've seen some of the most effective and brilliant ideas and interventions be overlooked or ignored for various, often well-intentioned reasons. Why educational institutions and clinical practitioners do not know more about the insights of individuals like Roberto Assogioli, Bob and Mary Goulding, Alexander Lowen, Stephen Karpman, Taibi Kahler, and hundreds of others is beyond me. (And I do not mean to slight the hundreds of other professionals I did not name who are every bit as insightful and articulate as those I did mention). But my point is that most readers of this book never heard of these people or of the thousands of ideas they have promoted that can improve individual and family life.

I don't understand why a "trickle down" process has not brought many tools and methods directing intentions into the living rooms of all families. It seems like they should be household words and games taught to children. I don't understand why so many psychotherapy clients and therapists, as well, do not know and cannot articulate more specific tools and methods. And, too, I don't know why they are not articulated and available in schools, churches, temples, mosques, and casual conversations. The techniques and tools are right in front of us everyday – yet far too often ignored.

Lacking clear and well articulated tools for growth, self-improvement, and health, people become *dis-empowered*. Those unable to escape through denial are taught to rely on pharmaceutical interventions. Most of my clients do not expect that there is anything they can do for themselves to become happier and healthier. I am asked questions like, "Can you cure depression?" "Can you fix my panic attack?" "Can you stop my anxiety problem?" "Can you work with bi-polar disorder?" And so on. Rarely, very rarely, am I asked, "Can you teach me how to solve my problem?" People are usually unaware of their own contribution to their personal problem or their family problem.

It saddens me that what is contained in this book is not common knowledge used by everyone on a daily basis. It is not too late to start. The tools in this book will change your experience and change your life. They must become strong habits in order to replace the strong habits that have previously been learned – habits that can lead to depression, anxiety, low self-esteem, poor performance, stress and energy depletion, conflict escalation, and the myriad of consequences these conditions create. Some of these tools will bring immediate consequence and some need to be repeated often for several days before the positive response reaches critical mass and becomes apparent. My goal is to make them now available and articulated with enough attention to detail that they can be easily

6 Tools to Express Intention

learned. Please use these tools for the maximum betterment of all concerned. That is, after all, the context in which they will work best.

In the end, our intention can be as automatic as breathing. These are the tools that help deliberately shape those experiences that can, with practice, eventually become automatic and unconscious inspiration.

3. Chunking Logic and Magic Markers

"Chunking logic" is an attitudinal approach towards daily experience. To understand it properly we first need some background information. In order to process any experience or encounter during our life we need to make sense of it and assign meaning to it. We need to put a frame around it – a frame that provides some sort of meaning. To use an exaggerated example, imagine that a giant floating yellow ball of gas suddenly appears in the middle of your backyard. And imagine further that you haven't even come to explain it as a giant yellow ball of gas that's floating. In other words, a very weird event occurs in your backyard for which at first you have no explanation or label. You would not know how to respond and you would not know what meaning to make of it. Illustration 1 shows how difficult getting an understanding of something can be when you can't relate it to something previously known or, in other words, you can't "frame" it. The mind is hardwired to send high voltage electrical spindles up the base of the brain when it fails to interpret an event within a given period of time. When that happens, a person will experience fainting, grief, fear, or anger. But prior to that, the brain has been in a hurry to make meaning of the event – and failed!

In a search to make meaning you will apply previous understandings that in some way seem parallel to the event. This process is basically an unconscious habit…although you may be

8 Chunking Logic and Magic Markers

aware of trying to figure something out. Thankfully, most novel experiences in our life seem to resemble some previous experience and therefore lend themselves to being understood. However, many people have a history of believing that a novel experience will be negative. Perhaps they have lived in families where they felt that nothing they did was considered correct. If they were active that was punished, if they were noisy that was punished, if they were excited about something that was met with suspicion or punishment, etc. These people have grown up learning to anticipate something negative about most situations they encounter.

Illustration 1: If it is too difficult to comprehend, it has no meaning to you because you can't find a "frame" for it. Without the frame it has no meaning.

When that has happened, every daily event is considered a negative experience. If a person wakes up late they may think, "Now my whole day will be ruined." When they realize that their gas tank is low they say, "Oh my gosh I might run out of gas before I get to work." When they see their supervisor noticing their late arrival they may think, "I'm in trouble again - she hates me. I'll never get the vacation time I want this summer." When they sit at a desk and see the material that awaits them for the day they may say to themselves, "I hate this job - I can never catch up." And this pattern continues throughout the day and night. Unfortunately, it continues day after day as well. The results of all of this negative thinking is likely to be depression, reduced energy, and a compromised immune system.

These are all examples of framing, or in other words, making meaning out of normal every-day events. The meaning that a person makes out of their life experiences is a matter of conditioning and habit. The origin of that conditioning is not really of importance to us. What is of importance is developing habits which will overcome that previous programming and conditioning so that we may experience life with more joy, creativity, and energy.

Goals for Chunking Logic

The tool of chunking logic amounts to deliberate acts of applying deliberate frames and deliberate meaning to everyday events so that people maximize their positive experiences, energy, optimism, creativity, and health. When we deliberately pay attention to daily events in the way we label them it is possible to develop new habits that overcome the previously relied upon negative thinking and perception.

Some people may argue that they are realistic in the way they label and interpret events. After all, a flat tire is a negative experience that delays our progress, makes us dirty, and costs us money. How could that be experienced as a positive moment in our life? People who consider themselves realists will insist that a negative interpretation of this event is absolutely appropriate.

My answer to such challenges is that we create social reality and we create the truth of our social reality. That is, if we choose to think that the flat tire is negative, it is in fact negative; if we decide to find a way to think of it as positive, it will in fact be positive. There are no objective criteria by which we can measure the effect these individual interpretations have on our lives. Each event of our life is a matter of interpretation. But the effect of a preponderance of negative or positive interpretation is a different matter. This can be measured. This concept is well known to researchers in relaxation and stress. Textbooks that discuss *stress* will tell you that similar events in the environment can occur to everyone and whether or not these are considered to be stressful to a particular person is a matter of the interpretation assigned to them by the individual. And, the effects of stress are emotional and familial, physical and medical.

Let me take the example further. A flat tire and how you fix it can be an experience that you frame as *positive*. For instance, you can be quite proud of the ability you have with tools, see how rationally you dealt with pulling the car off the road, assessing the situation, pulling the spare tire and jack from the trunk, and proceeding to fix it in an efficient manner (or, how calm you were as you called for your road service company). After all, there were times in your life when you did not know how one could perform a task like this. As an adult, however, you can take pride in the manner in which you are able to deal with such a common disruption in your schedule.

If you frame the experience of changing a flat tire as a positive experience you will have collected little or no stress from that incident. In addition when you think back over the events of the day you'll recall that you did something about which you are proud. So here is the question: Is it true that the flat tire was a dreadful nuisance, or is it true that changing a flat tire reminded you of your capabilities and how proud you can be about them? The answer is up to you. If you'd like to go through life collecting experiences of being a victim you will tend to favor the explanation that the flat tire was a dreadful inconvenience. If you'd rather go through life recognizing that you have a great deal of skill that makes you proud, you will favor the other explanation of the flat tire incident. Neither of them is true by any definitive or objective measure. Instead, either of them is true depending upon what you decide. In short, you get to decide whether your life is a series of positive experiences or a series of negative experiences.

The goal of operating with chunking logic is to give you an opportunity to label life events as positive or negative all day and every day. If you interpret most of your daily events as negative you can be fairly certain that you will become vulnerable to stress and, if this typifies your thinking, you may actually be clinically depressed. If you learn to interpret daily events as positive the opposite will be true - you will likely be stress free and happy.

In addition to chunking experiences as positive or negative, you can also chunk experiences as large or small. The following example may serve to illustrate this.

In Illustration 2 a mountain climber has suddenly found that a speck of dust blows into his eyes after accomplishing a climb to a high peak. The point of the illustration is that this event, like most events in our lives, can be interpreted as positive or negative and can be interpreted as very large and important or very small and unimportant.

Illustration 2: Placing flag in the mountain our hero gets a pebble in his eye!

- Chunking "+" Big: "Wow! The power of the Earth is amazing."
- Chunking "+" Small: "Oh, I'm glad I brought my goggles."
- Chunking "-"Small: "Gosh, you can get hurt by debris way up here."
- Chunking "-" Big: "Oh man! I come all this way and I get hurt...I'm such a loser."

Chunking an event as a small negative experience will lead you to tactics or strategies for change. Chunking an experience as negative *and* large will lead you to a negative belief system (e.g., a philosophy), and basically, an inability to change. For example, if a stone chips your windshield, you could chunk this *negative and large* by saying, "My car is a wreck." This sort of thinking can easily lead you to a further belief that, "Nothing ever goes my way." This is more philosophical and does not point toward a solution without much more effort.

However, if you were to say, "Oh there is a small chip in my windshield," this can easily lead to thoughts like, "I wonder who fixes those?" In this sequence your meanings easily lead you to an understanding that the windshield can be repaired. In other words, chunking negative experiences as *small* leads almost immediately to tactics for change and correction. On the other hand, chunking negative experiences as *large* leaves you essentially helpless.

The same concepts of chunking experiences negative applies to chunking experiences positive. In other words making an experience a *small* positive event makes it seem less important, easily overlooked and forgotten. Labeling events with a very *large* chunk of positive meaning makes them easier to remember. If a meeting goes well you have the option of saying, "that meeting went okay," and making it a positive chunk which is very small. You also have the option of saying, "People got a great deal out of what I had to say." In that event, the larger positive chunk of experience will stay in your memory longer. Remember, the goal of this tool is not to discover the most objective way to label reality but rather to find the most efficient and pleasant way to live.

It's necessary to point out that some events will be almost impossible to label as positive. The death of a loved one or a terrorist attack is a large negative experience. These sort of events may remain large and negative in our minds for long periods of time before they change. It's not appropriate to gloss over or whitewash obviously negative experiences. Doing that will only lead to eventual difficulties of all types – not the least of which will be a disconnect from others who do not share your opinion about these important incidents. However, most daily events are not nearly as life-changing as those. Most daily events are as mundane as being late, spilling your coffee, getting a spot on your shirt, failing to make someone laugh at your joke, having work that has to be taken home, and so on. These sort of daily events are hardly important enough to occupy a negative memory in our mind and certainly not important enough to occupy a large chunk of negative memory.

So the tool of chunking logic is simply that we learn to purposefully and deliberately apply positive interpretations to experiences throughout our day. Furthermore, it's most beneficial to find a way to make large chunks of positive experiences out of most events. And finally, when an event is considered to be negative, it is always best to decide to make it a small negative chunk of experience as those lead to tactics and strategies for change. This tool must be understood and then practiced until it becomes a habit.

Practicing Chunking Logic

Exercise One. A useful way to start applying chunking logic can begin immediately. If you are reading this, put it down for a moment. Look around. Listen. Recognize the degree of relaxation you feel right now. Become mindful of your breathing. Find something in your perceptual field – something you can see, hear, feel, smell, or any combination of senses – that you like. After all, if you are reading this things around you are likely to be rather calm. Notice the calm. Find the harmony. Enjoy looking at something you've been by passing in your busy days – a color, a shape, a reminder of a fun time, etc.

As you notice one or several of these be sure to add a positive interpretation...and in fact an interpretation that is even more positive than you are accustomed to assigning to the experience. Instead of saying, "Well at least I'm relaxed for a moment," think "It is fantastic to relax." Instead of thinking, "I like that color of blue," think "I really love something about that color." Find the thoughts and words that can work for you, of course, but always with the spirit of this chapter in mind. This is using chunking logic. Do this several times a day and continually increase your frequency of using it. Learn to do it more and more rapidly throughout the day. You can practice most anywhere at most anytime, which then makes it easier to do and leads to it becoming a habit. You will soon experience the benefits.

Exercise Two. Think back to a recent experience you took to be negative – not one of those life-changing problems – but a daily event. For instance, maybe a bowl broke in the microwave, or perhaps the boss just added a pile of files to a desk you had almost cleared off. It can be most anything you experienced as negative because the fact that you can recall it means you chunked it large! So think back to the events of the last day or two and pick only one with which to start.

Next, take an inventory of the words you used to describe it. You find things like, "it's terrible," "It kills me," "pain in the neck," "I can't live like this," "I can't take it," "it's a disaster," "it's ruined," "I can't believe it," "now I'm sunk," and probably a few expletives I don't need to put in print, and so on.

Take note of how remembering the event makes you feel. That is, as you recall these moments in more detail you should find yourself more worried, stressed, more emotional, and more tense. Go ahead and notice that the memory of the event *and* the meaning you gave to it results in feeling unpleasant. Try not to get caught up in it again, this is only an exercise and you have more steps to complete.

Now put your reaction aside and quickly do a bit of pretending. Imagine that some person who is cool, calm, and collected - someone unflappable like a James Bond or Jessica Fletcher from *Murder, She Wrote* – you can even use one of them if you like – encounters the same event. If you know real individuals who can serve as a model for calm, quick thinking, use the real person for this step instead. This need not take more than a few seconds in your imagination. As you think about the comments he or she would make you will also no doubt realize their characters would be more calm and collected than you. For the broken bowl, Bond might comment, "I better get that cleaned up before someone gets hurt because of it." For the pile of files added to his desk, he might say, "I see your confidence in my ability is very high as usual."

I'm not trying to trivialize or make silly and irrelevant interpretations to real problems with the above suggestions. Instead, I am urging you to realize that a person could conceivably stay much more calm and effective by making less exaggerated comments and reactive interpretations about difficult moments. For the sake of this exercise, take a moment to go so far as to amuse yourself with how such imaginary characters would be able to take the problems in stride.

Finally, by contrasting your real comments with those of the real or imaginary "ideal" model arrive at a few realistic comments you might have made instead of those you identified earlier. After recognizing the obvious difference in how he or she would have framed the event, imagine living through it again using words and reactions similar to theirs'. Notice how it makes you feel, and even think, differently than you did originally.

Doing this exercise twice a day, once at mid-day and once again at night, you will soon begin to form different expectations of your chunking habits for negative events. It is a simple matter of increasing the awareness of your options with comparison and contrast. Doing the exercise repeatedly will result in a halo effect. That is, you will begin to approach new problems with better chunking logic for longer and longer durations after the exercise.

18 Chunking Logic and Magic Markers

The combined effect of gathering even more positive experiences and having prolonged bouts of handling problems with small negative chunks will shift your habits of interpreting life. You will have made a habit of applying chunking logic. Your positive results at both of these exercises will slowly, at first, and then more rapidly gain momentum. Within a couple of weeks you should find that they reach a critical mass and your on-going daily experience profoundly improves. But don't relax back into old habits. Developing the habit of applying chunking logic is a life-style change. After all, you probably practiced the opposite for years. Plan on engaging in this as a new approach to living that you will utilize for years to come in order to feel, among other positive things, energized, happier, optimistic, and capable.

4. Self-Hypnosis

The goal of self-hypnosis is to create a relaxed physical state accompanied by a mental state of heightened concentration. This mental and physical state is possibly beneficial in and of itself if your aim is to dispel stress and help your body do the physical maintenance that accompanies relaxation. But it is better utilized as a tool. It is a means to an end. Just like a hammer is used for various purposes, hypnosis is a tool that is to be used for various purposes. The real benefit of self-hypnosis is the establishment of a state of heightened concentration that lays the foundation for several of the other tools of intention in this book.

How Self-Hypnosis works

Keep in mind that hypnosis, whether it comes from working with a mental health professional or on your own, is not what you may have come to learn from television and the movies. Real hypnosis is not a state like sleep, coma, or loss of awareness. Careful scientific research has repeatedly shown that hypnosis is more like the waking state than sleep. You don't "go deeply asleep" and you don't "wake up" from a hypnotic trance. You may have read about or heard a practitioner use those words, but they are not accurate. They mislead the public into thinking that hypnotic trance is like sleep. Other common myths are that hypnosis is a spooky state wherein you have no control, suggestions are implanted into your subconscious that you are duty bound to follow, a person becomes open to spirit possession, it leads to amnesia or being flooded with traumatic memories, it may result in being stuck in trance and unable to get out, and it can make you cluck like a chicken when you hear a bell ring. Unfortunately, many people think much of that is true. Fortunately, none of it is. But if you think any of it could be, stop reading now and skip to another chapter. Too many people fear what they do not understand and in the process invent all manner of far-fetched stories rather than investigate to learn the truth. If you are interested in investigating the science behind hypnosis I suggest you read issues of *The American Journal of Clinical Hypnosis*, or the *Journal of Clinical and Experimental Hypnosis*. These are the journals of the only two *strictly* professional organizations in the U.S. for health care professionals in medicine, social work, psychology, and dentistry. They contain clinical cases and empirical research from the world's top scientists, researchers, academicians, and clinicians on hypnosis, its proper application, and its results.

    Self-hypnosis is a process that will take only a few minutes to create. On the average, a session can last from a couple of minutes to up to 30 minutes. There has been some research that indicates you will come out of trance in about 30-40 minutes or less if you are uninterrupted. You can always bring yourself back sooner if you can't devote that much time to a particular session. Let's look at some methods so you can choose the ones that best suit you. Throughout this book exercises will call for relaxation and concentration, and while you need not use self-hypnosis to use those tools of intention, it is always an option for increasing your focus.

Self-Hypnosis 21

The primary goal for using this tool is to learn a method of self-hypnosis which allows you to establish and maintain physical comfort when you need to reduce stress. In addition it provides a method for mild anxiety control, pain management, and so on. Finally, it provides a method of self-preparation that allows you to keep a heightened focus while using other tools in this book.

Method 1: The funnel image

I refer to this first method as the "funnel image" because you use the pretense or image of sliding through a funnel or tube to reach deeper breathing and relaxation. Illustration 3 visually depicts the steps described below. If you repeat this several times in a row it can become a form of rapid self-induction.

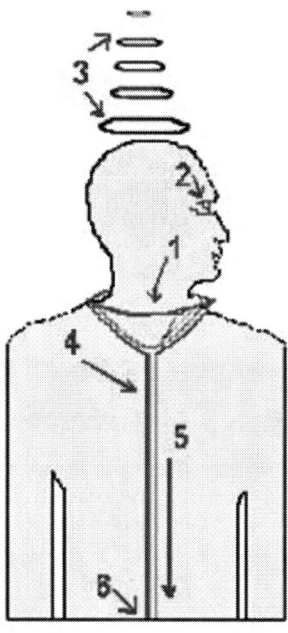

Illustration 3: The steps of the funnel self-induction

Step 1: Imagine or visualize a funnel which extends from the top of your neck to the bottom of your seat on the chair. Imagine the wide flange supports your head and the narrow tube descends down to the chair.

Step 2: Before you slide down the tube roll your eyes upward as if you are trying to see the top-most end of the tube.

Step 3: Imagine seeing the hole at the top of the tube get smaller in diameter as it gets further away as you go to step 4. Watch the top-most end of the tube get further away to help you feel step 4.

Step 4: Imagine that your center of gravity (or your eyes or what makes up "you") begins to slide or fall through the tube. Pretend this so well that you feel the actual but pleasant sensations of sliding down.

Step 5: Feel the sensation of sliding or falling as you imagine going down the tube and becoming more distant from the top-most opening. Finally, feel your gentle impact on the seat of the chair as you reach the bottom of the tube where you posterior end meets the chair with relaxation. You may notice that your breathing lowered and became abdominal breathing during this step.

Step 6: Feel the relaxation in the seat as you sit comfortably on the chair. Let the relaxation in that region of your body spread and at the same time "jell" in your body. This should take several breaths. You created this lowered breathing and relaxation by using your imagination. So, don't imagine anything else until this relaxation becomes solid in your experience (if you imagine something else, you will change the feeling).

Step 7: Now, retaining this comfort in your body, keep your eyes closed while you practice any of the other tools in this book that require comfortable, relaxed mental focus.

Method 2: The blackboard and stairway

A powerful method for creating self hypnosis can be created using our ability to visualize, talk to ourselves, and imagine changes in our feelings. This is a three part protocol that may require anywhere from three to ten minutes to complete. As with any of these protocols, this does not have to be done perfectly. It is the process of correcting your intention through these phases which creates the successful outcome. As a result, minor errors and omissions in the process will not prevent you from achieving positive results. However, as with any task, "practice makes perfect." The more easily you can succeed at these steps without pausing to correct yourself, the more profound the results will be.

Step 1: Find a comfortable place to sit and become mindful of your breathing. It is always recommended that self hypnosis be done in a seated posture keeping your back as straight as possible. If you are comfortable with a meditation posture that too is acceptable.

Step 2: Close your eyes and begin visualizing a blackboard in your mind's eye.

Step 3: Next, imagine yourself writing on this blackboard in the following way. You can see your hands writing on the blackboard (seeing in first person) or you can see your entire self writing on the blackboard (seeing yourself in the third person). What you write on the blackboard you will immediately erase (Illustration 4). Once you erase what you've written you will write the next item and then erase that.

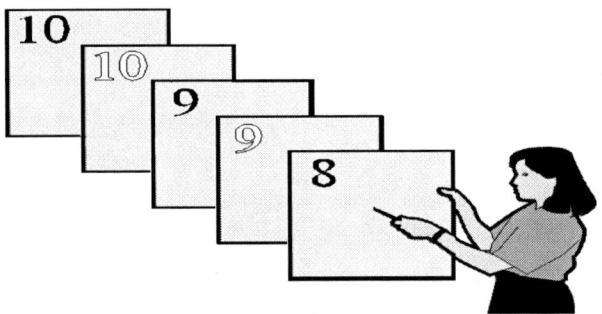

Illustration 4: Writing and erasing numbers on a blackboard.

The easiest method for conducting this protocol is to write the numbers from 10 to 1 on the blackboard - first visualizing them and then erasing them one at a time. Other options will be discussed shortly.

Step 4: After you have written and then erased the number one you will be looking at a blank board. Continue seeing nothing but that blank board and count backwards silently from 10 to 1. With each number, become more relaxed and allow your concentration to become more focused and internally absorbed. If you wish, you could silently comment after each number the phrase, "and becoming more deeply concentrated," or you may say, "going more deeply inside." For example, you would say to yourself, "10, and becoming more deeply concentrated," and then pause for as long as it takes you to inhale and exhale. Next, silently say to yourself "9, and becoming more deeply concentrated." Of course, you would continue this process until you have completed saying to yourself, "1, and becoming more deeply concentrated."

Step 5: Next, imagine that there is a stairway in front of you containing 10 steps going down. Standing at the top of the stairway begin descending onto the top (10th) step with either foot. Actually imagine the feeling that your foot and leg are moving. Imagine shifting your weight and moving your next foot down onto the step below. It may be necessary for you to do some minor self-talk to keep track of the number of steps that you are descending. That is perfectly all right. The main emphasis however is on your feeling that you are moving down the stairs one step at a time until you reach the bottom.

Step 6: Once you have reached the bottom of the stairs imagine that you become seated on a chair that's awaiting you. While you remain seated on this chair you can do any of the imaginary work described in the tools of intention listed in this book.

Step 7: When you are ready to reverse the process and end your self-hypnosis session you simply reverse the processes that brought you here. Imagine climbing up the 10 stairs, silently count from one to 10, and then count from one to 10 a second time (it is not necessary to again to visualize the process of writing these numbers on the blackboard). At the end of your second count to 10, open your eyes and return your awareness to the room. You may want to write down some of your thoughts so that you can review them later.

You might experiment with different outcomes that can be obtained during the visualizations in step 2. For instance, try writing the days of the week that lead up to the next weekend. Usually a weekend is a time when people have an opportunity to relax, so write the days of the week that lead to the next opportunity you will have to thoroughly relax. This can also be done with the months of the year leading up to your next vacation. Similarly, the year can be written on the blackboard and erased to create the experience of going back in time. That is, you would write the current year on the blackboard, then erase that year and write the year prior to it. Continue to write the previous year on the board until you arrive at the desired year for your purposes. You may want to recall a confident feeling that you had in college that occurred 15 years ago. If that is the case then you would continue to replace the year that's written on the board with the previous year until you reach that date when you were in college having those feelings. With minor modifications I think you can began understanding the flexibility that's possible with this second method of self hypnosis.

Method 3: Finger magnetism

The method relies upon your feeling sensation to lead you into hypnosis. While the title of this section uses the word "magnetism" to describe the method there is nothing magnetic that is really accurate in this activity. It refers instead to the feeling that you tend to get when you do the following activity. Begin by placing your fingers about one quarter to one-half inch apart and as you do, leave your arms and elbows suspended in the air. Hold this posture and relax for a few breaths. Soon you will begin to feel a tingling experience in many of your fingertips. At this point, if you move your fingers slightly closer and slightly further apart, there is an illusion of a magnetic attraction between your fingers. Again, this of course is not magnetism, but that is a colorful and descriptive name that allows you to remember this technique.

The feeling actually is a heightened sensitivity to the capillary pressure and the ends of your fingers. This can be a very useful feeling for developing heightened internal concentration and, hence trance. Your goal is to create this feeling and magnify it until you can shift your entire experience to resonate with it.

28 Self-Hypnosis

Step 1: Place both of your hands in front of abdomen without your elbows or forearms making contact with your lap. Line up the fingers of both hands so they are about one-quarter to one-half inch apart.

Step 2: Relax your arms and become mindful of your breathing until you can observe the jerky movements in some of your fingers and a feel a tingling or a pulsing in some of your fingertips. Move your fingers slightly closer together and further away from each other to accentuate the feeling (Illustration 5).

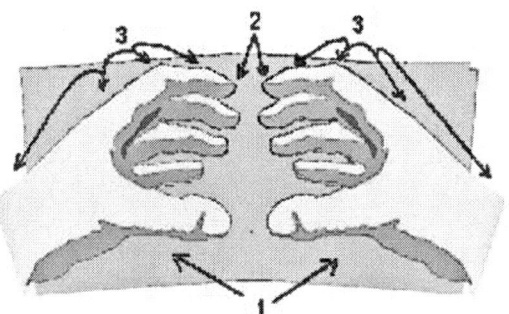

Illustration 5: Progressively move the sensations from fingers to arms.

Step 3: Holding this tingling or pulsing sensation in your awareness, turn your concentration to the next knuckle (toward your palm). Wait until the tingling or pulsing moves to that knuckle. Now, systematically repeat this concentration to each subsequent knuckle until the pulsing feeling follows each in turn. Eventually, you will find that the entirety of your fingers and even your hands and palms will resonate with this pulsation or tingly sensation.

Step 4: Continue this consciously "leading" of that sensation up into your forearms, elbows, upper arms, shoulders, and finally your neck. Take each wrist, elbow, shoulder joint slowly, one at a time. Within 2 or 3 minutes you are likely to feel that you have the full involvement of your fingers, arms, and neck.

Step 5: Surround the entire torso in this feeling, then continue moving it into the feet and finally, the head.

Step 6: Begin the use of other tools and protocols at this point.

Step 7: To terminate the exercise, open your eyes, take a couple of breaths and then shake-out the feelings from your hands and arms.

When you are done with any of the self-hypnosis sessions you may discover that you have experienced a loss of time or that more time passed on the clock than it seemed to you while you were in trance. Also, you may have a sense that you have forgotten some of the ideas and images that you created while you were in trance. Both of these are common and normal reactions to spending time with heightened concentration. However, if you do not have either of these experiences, that too is perfectly acceptable. They are not necessary for a self-hypnosis session to be successful and rewarding.

This state of heightened concentration reduces the number of distracting thoughts that a person might have while concentrating on a desired goal. This results in a stronger bond between associations that you make. For example, if you use the self hypnosis session to do self-image thinking protocol you might heighten an experience of confidence and imagine having that confidence at an upcoming staff meeting. When your concentration for the feeling of confidence contains little or no distraction, the ability to condition that feeling to occur during the sights and sounds of the staff meeting will increase.

To make this point, I often use the example of gluing two pieces of a broken cup together. In order to create a better bond you have to clean off the dirt from both edges making contact with one another. To the extent that you have successfully cleaned all of the oil, grease, dust, and dirt from the contact point, you will have a strong bond. On the contrary, to the extent that there are unnecessary pieces of dust and dirt on the edge, the glue will not bond to it firmly. In this metaphor, you're heightened concentration removes distracting thoughts from your experience and your anticipations. The distracting thoughts are like unwanted pieces of dust and dirt that only serve to weaken the bonds you're attempting to create. Thus, it seems to me that the use of self hypnosis to accompany the tools of intention in this book will invariably result in more rapid and enduring changes.

Don't despair if you wish to skip the section on self-hypnosis. All of the tools of intention can be successfully utilized by simply following the directions that are given in each chapter. It might be accurate to estimate that using any of them two times during self-hypnosis is approximately equivalent to doing them three or perhaps four times without self-hypnosis. Either way is just fine.

5. Appreciation Lists

It was mentioned previously that developing habits of "chunking logic" have a number of physical and psychological benefits. These, in turn, result in interpersonal and other benefits. In fact, everything in this book might be reduced down to one sentence: Collect, retrieve, and utilize positive experiences if you want to live a happier and more productive life. This chapter is about another powerful way to go about that - the use of "appreciation." Specifically, this is about collecting, experiencing, re-experiencing and using a sense of appreciation each day.

I have heard people shrug-off the notion of using appreciation and dismissing it as a silly idea, a waste of time, "simple positive thinking," and a "fine idea but it doesn't help." These criticisms and dismissals tend to come from individuals who are not happy, and for whatever reason, are using their minds in ways that contribute to their stress.

I've spoken with individuals who thought that the activity of listing appreciations was a type of penance. That is, a sort of "giving of the self" to make a concession. They stated that it felt like giving away a bit of themselves, like saying a "thank you" when they didn't really feel thankful. They seemed to think it was like being asked to conform for an arbitrary reason - that it is an act to be done for the benefit of others or to develop an understanding or empathy. But the main reason to practice this daily exercise is to develop a habit of retrieving positive experiences for your own health.

Often people believe that what they think and feel might only result in some sort of minor change, but getting the world (or other people) to change will result in a substantial change in how they feel. That is not the case. People exposed to the same situations have widely different responses. One person can take a trip to Disney World and have the best time of his or her life while another person with an almost identical background can find the trip burdensome and dreadful. It is not the change of environment, it is how you utilize your intentions when dealing with your environment that matters.

An appreciation is a favorable judgment or evaluation about an event or experience. It is the development of a sensitive awareness of something for which we are holding an aesthetic value. In addition, it is the expression of admiration, approval, or gratitude for that value and awareness.

Easy Method

The best time to review appreciations is before going to sleep each night, taking a moment to write out a short phrase or sentence for each item you appreciate.

>Step 1: (For unhappy people.) Think back through the day and identify a half-dozen events that in some way please you. If you have trouble finding something positive begin by thinking about things that didn't go as badly as they might have. For instance, you might recall that even though you broke a plate you appreciate that you didn't get cut; even though you had a flat tire, there was no traffic accident. Things

could have been worse. So if you are a person unfamiliar with gathering positive experiences throughout the course of a day begin by appreciating that things weren't worse for a half-dozen specific events.

Step 1: (For all others.) Think back through the day's events and identify a half-dozen specific moments that in some way please you. Later, you can increase this number to over a dozen, but at first begin small. The incidents you choose may have brought you joy at the time they happened. For example, you received a phone call that your son was hired for a great job he'd been hoping to get or maybe you ran into a dear friend in a restaurant. In these cases you already know how good you felt. However, the incident may have been one for which you did not take the time to savor the good feeling as it was happening. You might have participated in an informative lecture or perhaps you squeezed in time to fill your car with gas before work. Again, in these situations you may not have taken time to notice any good feeling whatsoever. You might not have thought to consider these positive times that were worthy of this exercise. Yet, they will work perfectly for our purposes.

Step 2: Dwell on each memory of each of the six situations, one at a time. In the case where you actually remember feeling good, make the memory as vivid as possible and recapture the good feeling. Now, while having the feeling, talk to yourself about it. Silently say things like, "that's great," "I love stuff like that," "that makes me feel good," and so on. Adding the self-talk may increase your absorption in the good feeling.

In the cases where you did not have a noticeable positive feeling during the actual event you proceed slightly differently. Once again begin by remembering the moment. But this time add the self talk first. And, in choosing your words, remember the chapter on "chunking logic." Now, *label* or frame the event to yourself in words as being more positive then it was as the time. You can use the same words that appeared in the last example. As you do, attempt to find the truth in them. You probably did not consider that filling the car with gas put happiness in your heart. However, it is entirely possible that once it actually did! I recall that each of my children felt a great deal of joy the first time they put gas in their very own car. That was probably true for each of us. So why did we lose track of that feeling when we fill our cars routinely? Perhaps it was the novelty that caused our first joy. But the same situation still exists: it is our car, we are able to put gas in it, and that is a real accomplishment (no pun intended).

So, why not appreciate the incident and feel good about it? It is worthy of appreciation.

Illustration 6: It is best to write the appreciation list.

Step 3: Write down a phrase for each of the things you identified and appreciated (Illustration 6). Don't worry if the list is 12 to 15 items or more in length. That will become customary, and it is appropriate. It is a good idea to keep the list by your bed (especially if you are performing this activity at bedtime).

Step 4: Upon awakening each morning, before rising from bed, try to recall the items you listed the night before. You will be surprised how many you fail to recall. Next, read the list of appreciations from the night before to refresh your memory.

This is a useful process to adapt for starting your activities every day. It help keeps you focused on the goal of being mindful of your life, your values, and the fact that you are surrounded with many options for good feelings throughout every day. It will make

36 Appreciation Lists

several other intention exercises in this book much easier to perform and to acquire as new habits.   This is most obvious for the tools of Vivid Symbolic Imagery, Self-Image Thinking, and for establishing Chunking Logic. If you begin and end each day mindful of a few positive experiences you are making a major contribution to your bank of positive experiences. And best of all, you are developing a habit that will snowball. Making appreciation lists will heighten your readiness to frame and "chunk" on-going events in a positive manner and recall them later for use in other exercises.

6. Vivid Symbolic Imagery

The goal of vivid symbolic imagery is experience retrieval. I can't emphasize enough that the goal of psychotherapy, medicine or personal growth in general, is to have the necessary resources you need in the context in which you need them. That principle is behind everything in this book. The tools of intention that people intend to develop are tools that will help them have the resources they need in the context they need, be it in the present or the future. So, many of the tools will continue to have as one of the primary goals - the retrieval or enhancement of experience. Some tools like self-image thinking utilize intention to associate desired goals with future situations. This tool, vivid symbolic imagery, is intended to strengthen the emotional and visceral experience of a desired goal. It can be done as a prelude to the long method of self-image thinking or simply done for its own sake. I recommend doing it for its own sake twice a day as a ritual designed to strengthen one's ability to experience and surrender to extremely important experiences. So important in fact, that these chosen symbolic images represent major life goals.

In order to accomplish this successfully with symbolic imagery you do not have to have an entire plan for your life goal. It's enough to understand that there are a handful of experiences which represent important paths in your own personal development. For instance, you may initially choose for important symbolic areas:

health, love, prosperity, and assisting others. For the sake of this example I will assume that those are the four areas that are relevant to you. However, at this point it is important that you actually decide what's important to you. It may be that what's most important to you is rising above some dramatic incident of the past, being assertive in your interactions, or having a degree of stick-to-it-iveness or perspicacity for a job that lies ahead.

Method for Vivid Symbolic Imagery

Step 1: The first step is to select those goals that are relevant to you. I would not advise you as an initiate to select more than three or four of these major goals. As mentioned above, these will be goals that are pertinent to you at this time in your life and for some months or years to come. These are different from the goals you might select in the chapter on self-image thinking which has to do with more immediate and transient experiences and goals. The items you are determining at this point are items that are essential for your maturation and growth, and for your happiness and well-being. That is not to say that these will be out of line with any of the other goals from other chapters, it is simply that these will *symbolically* represent the direction and path that you are intending to create for yourself (Illustration 7).

Vivid Symbolic Imagery 39

Illustration 7: A vivid symbolic image will act like a magnet to retrieve desired feelings

Step 2: The next step is to take each of these three or four areas one at a time and find a memory from your past that reminds you of a time you most successfully and most satisfyingly were working to accomplish the goal. For example, if one of your major areas of development is health, recall a time when you felt that you were eating healthy, or exercising regularly, or being the most mindful of your health, or so on. Perhaps you will remember a time when you, at least for a short while, were doing all of these things. It may have been back in high school, it may have been a time when you were in graduate school, it may have been 20 years ago or it may have been three years ago - it doesn't matter. What matters is that you can recall a time in your life where you did something that represents the area of your life you wish to recapture and continue to develop.

Step 3: The next step is to select some slice of that memory. By selecting a slice of the memory I mean take a small snapshot of any portion of that memory that seems the most appealing to you. It could be a time when you sat in the library reading a book about nutrition. Another example might be that it was a time when you awoke and put on your jogging clothes and jogged in adverse weather conditions. Maybe it was a time when you were a practicing vegetarian. It might be as minor as a time when you realized you were satisfied with what you ate and pushed away your plate rather than consuming every remaining morsel. There is no criteria that exists outside of your own sense that the memory, for you, represents your best effort to move in the direction in which you wish to grow and change.

Step 4: The next three processes constitute a single step. They may actually seem somewhat unnecessary. However, each part is important for specific reasons.

  a. The first of these three parts is to extend your arms and place your hands in front of you so that your elbows are not touching anything. Keep your hands separated about seven to 7 to 9 inches

Vivid Symbolic Imagery 41

apart – palms facing each other. Now relax. This will create a sensation where you can feel a sort of energetic connection between your hands. Some people describe this as sort of the magnetic feeling or pulsation between their hands. However, I believe that the entire experience is simply a matter of becoming more aware of or sensitive to the capillary pressure in your fingers and palms. Whatever the case, this experience is a body experience. That is, it is a visceral or proprioceptive experience. And that is the important part of this step.

b. The next part is to begin visualizing the image selected earlier as if it is taking place between the palms of your hands. In other words, make the image fit into the seven or eight inch area between your palms. Imagine that you see yourself in third person engaged in the activity that represents your desired goal. If your desired goal included being healthy, and your identified experience was a time when you were reading a book at the library on nutrition, then see yourself in the library sitting at the table reading that book.

c. The final part is to make the image as vivid as possible. Notice your face in detail, notice your shoulders, your body, your hips, your arms, the way your legs are, the way your feet are on the floor, even what you are wearing. It is important to try to make every aspect of this image vivid. You'll notice that there is a tendency to sort of generalize what you're seeing rather than seeing it. However the goal of this exercise is to create a vivid symbolic image.

Finally, continue to increase the lucidness of this image until you begin to get the feeling that you once had when you were in that situation. Don't be afraid to let the feeling actually move you. It should actually change your breathing, change your posture somewhat, and put a smile on your face. That is your goal. You are attempting to remember this experience in such detail that it drives your motor behavior, that it creates an actual visceral or feeling experience in your body.

It will probably be necessary to repeat this exercise a couple of times a day for about four days before you will finally feel the strong emotional/visceral experience. And when you do experience it emotionally it will have a very strong fixation on that symbolic image and the feeling that you're having. You'll be surprised to discover that you actually still have the feelings that go along with the incident you are picturing. I can't emphasize this enough: Repeatedly doing this vivid symbolic imagery will result in a change in your sense of capability. Within four or five days of doing this exercise in earnest, you will recognize that you actually are the person who has these feelings and they are not a thing of the past.

Obviously, feeling that these desired emotions and motivations are not a thing of the past but rather, are a part of the present, helps keep you on your intended path. It's mentioned above that you should have three to four of these symbolic images. Each day, during the two sessions in which you practice this tool of intention, you should spend two or more minutes on each of the symbolic images that you identified in step one. Again, for the beginner I recommend using no more than three or four symbolic images. Once your concentration and lucid visualization of these symbolic images can reliably create the desired feeling for you, the exercise can be completed in a matter of a few seconds. After that, it should be possible for individuals to do this vivid symbolic imagery exercise several times a day.

It should be noted that the symbolic images you initially chose may change slightly over weeks or months of doing the exercise. However, the goal or path that they symbolize will probably not change for several months or years. Typically, you will begin to recall other images that also symbolize the targeted experience. When that happens you can choose either to keep the original image, add the others to it as you fixate on it, or even alternate which symbolic image you choose to meditate on in a session.

Finally, it's important to remember that even though it becomes easy to create the feeling that these images symbolize the exercise should not be discontinued. These are tools for using your will and intention to organize and facilitate your deliberate development in the way you intend. The process of overcoming and replacing your default and previously learned programming requires that you deliberately create habits to experience needed emotions and attitudes and continue to do so until they become a lifestyle change (and therefore become unconscious habits).

You will find that after a session or two the VSI exercise will reliably create your desired feeling. You might reflect on this and think, "I *can remember* that feeling." But within a couple of weeks of practicing you will find that it feels deeper and think, "I *have* that feeling." However, after a month or two of practicing the VSI protocol a deep sense will develop and you will begin to *identify with* the experience it represents so strongly that your thoughts are liable to become, "I feel like I (still) *am* that person." In other words, the feeling first becomes a memory, then a experiential option, and finally a self-image.

7. Heart Joy

The lyrics of a popular song starts with "put a little love in your heart" and countless other songs suggest that we should speak from our heart, have a full heart, and of course avoid a broken heart. Unfortunately, it appears that many people think these are only poetic phrases and do not make a conscious effort to put joy in their hearts. But, they do put fear, anger, and sadness in their hearts. During highly charged times of extreme emotion, our heart rate quickens; we can feel our heart pound. This awareness subsequently associates any strong emotions, including the feeling of fear, anger or sadness, with our heart. For example, in a fit of anger a father shouts at his child and all he can be aware of is seeing his son, hearing his own raised voice, the rise of his emotion, and his pounding heart. Or, a child is afraid of being beaten and all he can experience is trying to hold his breath, a screaming parent, violent movements, the pounding of his heart, and his terror. When these experiences are numerous they interfere with fulfilling the motto of the love song.

Others have armored their hearts off with chronic muscle tension in their chest and by means of this protective defense they never experience any emotion associated with their heart. They are cold and detached from others. These individuals literally have formed a permanent muscular defense that inhibits their breathing. When strong tender emotion builds the body requires a rapid increase in oxygen. That breathing process is disallowed and, presto!, the tender feelings are stopped. Once this protective maneuver is learned the individual will find it helpful to avoid pain, humiliation, punishment, and so on, in the future. It will be used for years and eventually become an unconscious habit that the individual carries into adulthood. In any event, the bottom line is that these individuals do not have a feeling of joy associated to their hearts.

A Solution Emerges

I formulated and began using this exercise with clients after a successful session in 1995. My client was a woman who had been a Catholic nun for 36 years. She was depressed, overweight, and extremely self-sacrificing. She had many problems in her family of origin (e.g., including incest rape) that had influenced her decision to become a nun. Nowhere had she been encouraged to retrieve positive and satisfying experiences. She later told me that prior to this exercise she had never understood or believed the promises of peace and comfort her sisterhood offered.

At the beginning of the session the client reported that she had just completed a process in her church that had taken several years. I inquired as to how she celebrated and she told me that she did not celebrate and in fact I was the only person with whom she had shared the news. What followed, for her, was a self-reported religious experience. She insisted that she had not felt love in her heart prior to the experience that resulted from this exercise but would be able to do so again at any time of her choosing in the future.

Following that powerful outcome I used the protocol with subsequent clients. Whenever I did, I referred to it as "putting love in your heart" – a name that I knew would raise eyebrows and cause some to roll their eyes in at the pretentious label. Eventually, the term "heart joy" evolved as a more palatable name for the exercise I am about to describe.

I became optimistic that repeatedly associating joy with the sense of your heart would potentially yield health benefits. I would love to see a few thousand people participate in a longitudinal study compared to a matching control group. The experimental group would spend ten minutes a day with this exercise and the control group would simply sit quietly for ten minutes a day. I am so confident in this exercise that my estimation is that over the course of two decades the experimental group would display a history of greater cardiac health (i.e., fewer heart attacks, lower blood pressure, lower incidents of arterial trouble, and so on). Perhaps I can only wish for such spectacular research to be conducted.

However, in the Spring of 2008 I was teaching in the Northeast at a major psychotherapy conference and a participant said that my heart joy protocol was similar to that of an organization called HeartMath[1]. Further, the company had an advertising display booth in the vendors' hall of the hotel where the conference was being conducted. Speaking with them and looking into their biofeedback equipment I was impressed that they have been researching a remarkably similar protocol. Among their reported results, if I understood correctly, are decreased levels of the stress hormone cortisol and increased production of immunoglobulin IgA beginning within minutes after the achievement of the last step of a

---

[1] Childre, D. & Martin, H. (1999). *The HeartMath Solution*. San Francisco: Harper.

procedure they call "Freeze Frame." Readers can investigate this company and evaluate their research for themselves.

If these outcomes of increased immune activity and lowered stress hormones are, in fact, added rewards for this tool of intention I call "Heart Joy" I couldn't be happier. Whatever the case, the following steps of the protocol can be easily learned by readers.

Protocol For Heart Joy

There are three experiences that have to be associated. I do not think there is a correct order to proceed with retrieving and associating these target experiences. The following order of steps works best for me and seems to be the easiest or smoothest order for my clients.

> Step 1: Begin with the self-hypnosis protocol of your choice and proceed to the next step as indicated in that chapter or simply sit and become mindful of your breathing. If you haven't done so before now, attempt to breathe evenly through both nostrils. After you have slowed your breathing take at least a half-dozen breaths. Find pleasure in the mindful breathing and let that emerge into the foreground of your experience.
>
> Step 2: Using one of the memories that created a feeling of appreciation from the "Appreciation List" protocol let the feeling penetrate deeply and fully saturate your awareness. Let it bring a smile to your face. Basically, if it does not bring a smile to your face you need to use a different memory. This can be a

feeling of joy or love or pleasure from any of your memories. It can be a feeling that arises from your work with the "Vivid Symbolic Imagery" protocol.

It is okay to choose an experience that comes from a memory of a solitary or an interpersonal event. It would be more beneficial if you pick a positive experience that is not a result of competitive performance but rather the result of more cooperative interactions. If this step is difficult you need to revisit the chapter on "Chunking Logic" and do more work to implement that material into your daily life.

Hold the dual awareness of the pleasure of breathing with the feeling of appreciation, love, or joy. With both experiences in your awareness take several breathes before moving on to the next step.

Step 3: As you remain relaxed in this state of concentration try to find your pulse. You may locate it in your neck, ankles, wrists, or elsewhere. Using that rhythm as a guide, concentrate on your chest to find your heartbeat. Once you have connected with the feeling of your heartbeat continue to hold all three experiences in your awareness for a few minutes at each setting.

There are some options at this point. You can entertain yourself during the passing time by letting any one of the 3 experiences (pleasurable breathing, heartbeat, and feelings of joy or appreciation) move into the foreground of your awareness. As any one of those experiences become focal let the other two fade into the back of your mind. Then repeat with another of the three experiences into the foreground while a different combination moves into the background. Continue this alternating awareness for five to ten minutes.

One of the pitfalls that can influence the outcome of this exercise is the context of the memory you choice to generate a positive feeling. In my experience the best results come from choosing a memory that did *not* arise from an activity that was a performance or a competition. That is, the positive feeling that might come from winning a marathon is not as useful for this Heart Joy tool as the positive feeling that comes from being captivated by a sunset. I suspect that the crucial determinant is found in how the memory stimulates the parasympathetic nervous system. A completive feeling will trigger a heightened adrenalin response that is antithetical to our goal of calmness.

Once the three steps of the method are initiated and held in awareness for a dozen or so slow breaths it becomes possible to clear your mind of the antecedent memory. Attempt to reach this state and stop self-talk and visual imagery for the duration of the session. If possible, formulate a memory of your experience at that stage of development with the additional goal of recognizing and recalling it at will. This will make it easier to practice for ten minutes twice or more per day.

8. Self-Image Thinking

There is a card trick performed using the "Svengali Deck" that is a real crowd-pleaser, as they say. An apparently normal deck of cards is shown to the audience and an audience member is asked to cut the deck or call for the performer to stop flipping the cards at a random point. When the cut or flipping is stopped the next card is, say, the eight of clubs. The eight of clubs is then removed. That alone is not too impressive the first time...but as the performer stops or cuts the deck repeatedly, the same card - the eight of clubs - is *always* the next card – even though it is repeatedly removed! This effect can be repeated more than a dozen times. Yet each time, the flipping of the cards of the deck continues to show a set of random cards and each time the eight of clubs can be again removed. In summary, the effect is that the audience is shown a deck of cards and it is cut at random. Over and over the same card appears (despite the fact that it was apparently removed in the previous cut).

This card trick works the way *memory* works. However, the audience seldom understands the connection until they are told. Here's the connection: Sorting through your memories, your mind will bump into the large chunks of memory. If your large memories are negative and your positive memories are small, you will be

---

The material in this chapter was originally discussed in Lankton, S. & Lankton, C. (1983). *The Answer Within*, pg. 325-331; and, Lankton & Lankton (1989). *Tales of Enchantment,* pg. 216-257.

depressed and lack the resources for success. The card trick is analogous: There are 52 cards in the deck but the eight of clubs is every other card and there are 26 of them. The other 26 cards are random. But the trick is that the normal (random) cards are slightly larger than the 26 eight of clubs. As the performer thumbs and displays the cards the short (eight of clubs) cards fall face down against the random card. They do it so quickly they can't be seen. The "flip-displayed" deck appears to be random cards with no eight of clubs. Yet there are 26 of them!

Imagine that the memory of your life is just the same. You could have half of your life very negative and half of your life very positive. I suppose that statistically that might be about right. Yet, if you chunk the many positive experiences as insignificant and the fewer negative experiences as Earth shattering, you will only recall the large negative experiences when you reflect on your life. Alternately, if you categorize the positives as very significant and therefore large chunks of experience and you reduce the significance of the negative times, you will be happy and confident as you reflect on your life.

Only your large memories will stand out. These can be the negative or the positive memories. It is up to each person. And, as mentioned, most events lend themselves to either interpretation. There are always four possibilities: large or small positive and large or small negative labeling and interpretation of events. This may sound familiar because I have explained the ramifications of this in the chapter on Chunking Logic. We are revisiting it, however, because your habit in chunking life-experiences has a direct bearing on how you formulate your self-image and intent to act. Your intention to act is driven by your self-image.

Faced with any task or future event your mind sorts through what it knows about the situation. It does this at lightning speed and a portion of the result of the search often quickly emerges into awareness (e.g., opinions and feelings about the task or event). Remember, when you sort through your memories you bump into the larger ones – positive or negative. You think of yourself as strong, capable, happy, fun, and so on, or you think of yourself as confused, incapable, weak, lonely, depressed, and such. Whichever group of experiential memories is larger leaves its impact on how you define who you are and what you are capable of doing. This is your self-image. An unexamined self-image will operate below consciousness.

Self-Image Thinking is a tool for directing your intention so as to deliberately build a congruent and true self-image and replace bad habits that perpetuate old, unexamined and negative self-image thinking. For instance, consider what happens if Mona is depressed and a friend suggests going to a party. Mona thinks about the prospect of attending and "realizes" she won't enjoy it. She will opt to avoid the party. If she does, she will collect another bad feeling or reinforce her opinion that she can't have fun at parties. If, instead, Mona happens to go to the party anyway, she will most likely not enjoy it – just as she predicted. Again, she collects another bad memory and feeling. All of these will be used by Mona again in the future - in sort of a snowballing effect the past creates more of the same in the present – and the present is used to create the future.

This is why Mona's explanation is not as simple as it seems on the surface. Here is how it really happened. When Mona was presented with the option to go to the party her mind rapidly sorted through her relevant memories and found a preponderance of negative experiences. Some residual experiences made it to her awareness and she felt unhappy or depressed in various ways. With those feelings in her mind she anticipated the party scene and in that moment associated (or conditioned) her negative experiences to her imagination of the party. That is, she linked most of her perceptions of the party to her bad feelings. She created her future. When she eventually went to the party, voila!, her mind served up the bad feelings she had linked to the people and things she anticipated and she felt bad. In other words, she did not originally "realize" she would not enjoy the party as she thought – instead, she inadvertently used her self-image to insure her unhappy time by the act of creating a conditioned link by means of her self-image.

This is the on-going process that re-creates depression for people every minute of every hour of every day. When people learn to change the type of feelings they use with this predictable process they will change their depression. But while this is a terrific example of how people perpetuate their depression it is also an analogy of something we all do. It represents the same process used by all of us every day. Many people do not restrict themselves to using a self-image of depressed feelings when they anticipate the future. Some people use more colorful feelings including excitement, joy, loneliness, anxiety, kindness, courage, and so on. And whatever feeling they use, that is what they will experience in the future (barring some unforeseen circumstance that creates an unexpected reaction, of course). One thing people have in common is the process they use: retrieve experiences, hold them, and anticipate feeling them in a future event. And, also, most people use unexamined self-images built upon experiential memories they have not deliberately chosen and which often fall short of their best options.

The tool of Self-Image Thinking is intended to deliberately make use of that natural associational process of the mind and to eventually make a habit of this useful technique. There are two major parts of the tool: Central Self-Image building and Scenario rehearsals. What follows first is an articulation that is intended to be fool-proof by its level of detail. Once you become familiar with it you can shorten many of the steps for convenience and speed. I call the shortened version "Magic Markers." The entire process can easily and rapidly be utilized throughout the day.

Phase 1: Central Self-Image (CSI)

The first phase of the process is to deliberately create an image of yourself that represents you while you are experiencing a set of your desired attitudes and feelings. The visual image will serve as a mediation device between the intentions of the conscious mind and the resources that can be made available from learned unconscious experience. After the image is created it can then be used for a variety of scenario rehearsals. These constitute the second phase of the protocol.

Step 1: The first step in creating a Central Self-Image is to decide upon which experiential resources are necessary for the rehearsing you intend to do.

Usually three to six experiences are sufficient and appropriate. For example, a person may choose an experience where they felt confidence, smart, caring and compassionate, or optimistic. Please note, these four experiences are entirely arbitrary and being used for illustration purposes only. In actuality, users may choose any unique experiences that are necessary for the task at hand.

Step 2: The next step is to create a rudimentary visual image of yourself as you are at this time. This image does not have to be a lucid visual image. It is enough that you have a sense of seeing yourself ever so vaguely. It is not the degree of vivid visual detail that is necessary, but rather the fact that you are attempting to stimulate your internal visual imagery that is important. However, the greater degree of relaxation you obtain the better the visual image may be. And the more vivid the image is the easier it will be for you to add to and modify that form of visual thinking.

Step 3: The third step in the process of creating a Central Self-Image is repeated for each of the desired attitudes and feelings that you selected in step one. What is necessary is to recall memories of times when you had each experience, one at a time, and do so in a particular way. Beginning with your first desired resource stated in step one (confidence), remember a time that you had that experience. This memory does not need to have any relationship to an upcoming event in which you wish to have that confidence. In fact, it's most likely that your memory of having the experience of confidence will be in an entirely different context. This is how it should be. Having identified set memory, enhance all aspects of it until it becomes increasingly real to you. Remember where you were, remember the temperature, and remember who was with you. Remember how it smelled, the weight of the air you felt, and remember the rhythm of speaking or movement that was occurring. Remember what was in focus, remember the colors, and remember the sounds and conversation that occurred during the time you had that experience. Continue this sort of revivification until you have almost put yourself back into that early memory. Continue to do this until you have the feeling that occurred in that original situation. Once that feeling is again being experienced, let it spread over your body and on to your face as much as possible. Notice what changes occur in your face and body.

As you recognize the small changes that occur in your face and torso when you feel the positive feeling, make small changes to the visual image of yourself that you began to create in step two (Illustration 8). That is, to modify that small picture of yourself so that an observer would have the impression that the person they are seeing is having your desired experience. More specifically, if you got the feeling of confidence and noticed that your shoulders relaxed and there were small smile lines around your eyes make these changes to the visual image as well. In other words, use your own physical experience to make modifications to your visual image.

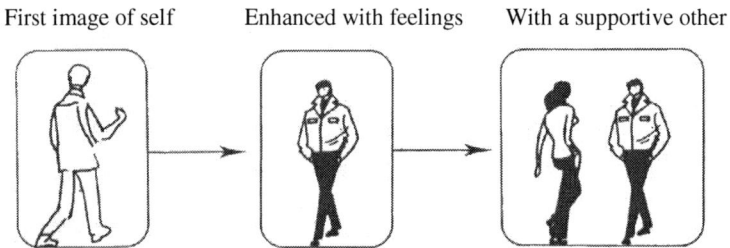

Illustration 8: A Central Self-Image is formed by adding visual indicators of desired resources to an image of yourself. Finally, an image of a supportive/reinforcing person is added to the CSI.

Now repeat this process of finding a memory, making it vivid enough to have the feeling, and modifying the visual image to be in keeping with that feeling. Each time you repeat the process select a different one of your initial desired experiences from step one. After you have modified that image to reflect all of the positive attitudes and feelings be certain that seeing that picture will allow you to also have those attitudes and feelings. Note that both the picture and your

Self-Image Thinking 59

own physical experience will be a composition created as a group or set of all the selected desired feelings and experiences from step one.

Step 4: The final step of this first half of the protocol is to slightly modify that image of yourself with the desired feelings. The modification simply needs to consist of adding another person to that image so that you can imagine interacting with that person. Make certain that the person you add is a supportive person. A supportive individual may be a parent, child, a friend, or even a religious leader or spiritual icon. What is necessary is simply that you add to this initial image a symbol that represents interaction and movement while maintaining these desired feelings. With the addition of another person your mental apparatus is established for the next process – rehearsal by means of visual scenarios.

Phase 2: Scenarios

This scenario rehearsal stage of the protocol consists of very simple steps. The first phase of this process involves building a Central Self-Image. Now take that Central Self-Image that represents your desired experiences, and *while keeping your desired experiences in your body* as you make the picture, change the background of this image so you can imagine acting in some future situation. For example, if you chose the four previously defined desired feelings, keep those present in your experience while you sit

60 Self-Image Thinking

and picture yourself with those desired experiences in the picture. I will emphasize this one more time: *It is absolutely essential that you keep the desired feelings in your awareness as you proceed.* You will have a physical feeling of the experiences and you will have a visual picture of yourself with experiences.

> Step 5: With that arrangement in place, let the background of that visual image change so that you see yourself interacting in some future situation where you want to have these desired feelings.

This is roughly depicted in illustration (9) below.

Illustration 9: The background of the Central Self-Image fades into a visual rehearsal.

For our example let's say that you want to have the feelings of confidence, being smart, being compassionate, and being optimistic in a future situation that involves making a presentation at a staff meeting. In the first part of this process you created an image of yourself with those desired experiences and you were able to use your memory to bring those experiences into your feelings while you built the picture. Now modify that picture of yourself with those four feelings so you see yourself at the staff meeting. Make certain you keep the feelings constant in your body as you watch yourself with the feelings in the staff meeting. Watch yourself and listen to yourself speak in this rehearsal. During the rehearsal notice who you see, what you hear, what you might touch and feel in that future staff meeting. Each of the things you imagine in the future can become triggers for you to have these desired feelings in that future context. The more accurate and detailed you are with your imagination of the future situation the more strongly you will have used your intention to condition or train yourself to have these desired feelings in that situation.

There is only one major difficulty a person might encounter at this stage. That difficulty is that you may not be able to see yourself in the future situation as you desire. This is the result of not having placed all of the necessary experiences in the original picture. Here is an example. A client came to see me because she did not feel that she was assertive enough to have her ex-husband served with a restraining order. When she built her Central Self-Image she placed many logical experiences in the picture. Once she had created a Central Self-Image of herself being strong and assertive and taking care of herself, etc., she began rehearsing the scenario of calling the police while her ex-husband was visiting her home. In the process of rehearsing that future situation however, she suddenly began to look very weak. I asked her why she had stopped holding on to her desired feelings and she replied, "all of my friends think that my life is perfect and I would be so embarrassed if they realized the truth." In other words, while she had acquired all of the assertive and courageous experiences she needed to confront her husband and call the police, she had left out one very important additional feeling resource. That is, she needed to have a sense that her friends would accept her even knowing about her domestic difficulty. At that point I had her stop this scenario and go back to Central Self-Image building. She needed to have a feeling of being accepted by her friends as part of that Central Self-Image. Once she had added that image to the others, she returned to the rehearsal of calling the police. At that point she had no difficulty completing this scenario and feeling that she had done the right thing.

The point of that example is to illustrate that a scenario will be successful and will associate you to your positive feelings unless an essential feeling has been left out of the original self-image. If in the process of rehearsing a future scenario with your desired experiences you find that it becomes difficult to hold on to the positive feelings you desire, ask yourself what additional feelings are necessary so that you can succeed at this task. If any additional experiences are needed one simply returns to step two and three of the first part of this protocol.

What happens if you are under the impression you have never had the desired experience needed for a particular task? The answer is often easier and less complicated than it would seem. There are two simple ways to proceed in a case like this. The first way is to recall an image of someone who has had the feeling you desire to have. You may have some friend or colleague who embodies the feeling or attitude you desire to have. In that case the central self image can be built using a feeling that can be obtained from your imagination of what it would be like to be that person while having that desired feeling or attitude. That is, if you've seen a friend be courageous at some point in time and stand up for him or herself in a situation, you can imagine being that person in that situation. Vividly making that image will produce a feeling in you that is similar to the one your friend would have likely had in that situation. A second way to proceed if you are under the impression that you do not have the desired feeling that is needed, is to realize that you may have actually had the desired feeling and failed to notice it at the time. A very common example occurs with the feeling of being safe. Let me give you an example, almost everyone has had the experience of sitting in a bathtub or swimming in a swimming pool. And at those times, the person is usually having an experience that could be called "safe." (The assumption is that a person would not stay in a bath tub or swimming pool very long if he or she didn't feel safe.) However, failing to have actually labeled the experience they may have grown up and concluded that they never felt the feeling of being safe. In fact, they did feel safe, however, they simply failed to label it and, consequently, failed to savor it. In other words, search your experience for times when you actually may have had an opportunity to feel your desired feeling even if you failed to label it that way at those times.

Summary of Long Method

The previously explained method illustrates the long method of employing this self-image thinking protocol. These steps can be summarized in the follow outline.

- Create a "Central Self-Image"
    1. Make a visual image of yourself to be used in the exercise
    2. Make a list of the desired resources that seem to be needed
    3. Retrieve the desired resources one at a time by revivifying memories
    4. Add each feeling resource to the picture (so the image reflects it)
    5. Make the image a social image by adding a supportive person to it
- Create and play "Scenarios"
    1. Let the background of the CSI fade into a scene
    2. Rehearse it through a gradient of easy to hard
    3. Continue to feel the desired resources in yourself
    4. Keep desired resources in CSI
    5. Run scenes to the end
    6. Add any additional resources that may be needed
    7. Add dialogue or narration as you watch the rehearsal

I recommend doing this long method for every one of the important and major events that occur in your life. Using this self-image thinking repeatedly on a regular basis for any event which is in the distant future will greatly enhance your ability to program your own experience and become well-conditioned. Of course as you approach the original distant event it is important to continue to use self-image thinking repeatedly for the desired feelings you wish to have during that event. Keep in mind that these events do not have to be performance oriented events. These can be trips with your family for a vacation. You might say that a depressed person does this very thing on a regular basis. The depressed person will take their bad feelings and while they are feeling them, they will imagine themselves in some future event. Of course they'll say that they'll feel bad if they go to that future event. If for some reason they are coerced into attending this event that they have already decided will result in bad feelings, it turns out that they are correct. They will have bad feelings. The bad feelings that they had were not something they correctly predicted, but rather, and this is very important, they are something that they programmed and conditioned themselves to have with their own deliberate intention. Basically, without realizing it, their anticipation of future events during a time when they felt bad created a conditioned response or a self-programming to have those bad experiences during the times that they live those events. They anticipated the sights and sounds and activities of a future event while they were feeling the bad feelings of depression. In doing that, they actually did a rough version of self-image thinking, only they did it with undesirable feelings. The fact that they succeeded fabulously attests to the importance of doing self-image thinking deliberately and doing so with desired feelings. It also attests to the fact that, just like the depressed person gets great results being depressed by thinking about these things regularly, thinking about having the desired feelings in future events will result in having desired experiences in the future. The more often you practice self-image thinking, the stronger your chances are of having those intended desired feelings be an automatic conditioned and programmed response in the future situations. It is that simple.

Short Method: "Magic Markers"

The short method for using self-image thinking is an adjunct to successfully using the long method. Once the long method has been accomplished for any desired future situation, an additional tool of intention can be used. This short method amounts to something that takes no more than one to two seconds of time throughout the day. Let's assume that you have already completed the long method of self-image thinking for an upcoming event. Now while you are being mindful of using chunking logic in the course of your day you may pick up a very desirable pleasant feeling. I call these "magic markers." It may be as simple as the good feeling that you have when you smell freshly cut grass while mowing the lawn. When you have that momentary good feeling that is a result of making a positive chunk of experience in daily events, immediately visualize yourself in the future scenario. That is, you're basically using your mind to direct your attention to have that positive feeling available in that future situation for which you've done a long version of self-image thinking. It's as if you're saying, "I would like to feel this good also in that future situation." In fact, making such auditory self statements as you visualize and feel your intention is a very good idea. Learning to have the desirable experiences in every sensory system will only strengthen the learning and make it more durable.

9. Future Shaping: Emanated-Images

Future Shaping Emanated-Images create presuppositions of success. When you presuppose something, you will find that it appears to "be true" or "come true." That is, the world seems to match our presumptions. Well, not our presumptions, exactly...our presuppositions. They are quite different. Consider the difference. A *presumption* is a type of cognitive conclusion or anticipation. It is a belief formed by some evidence that provided some probability for our conclusion. A *presupposition*, on the other hand, is what is called an antecedent – it was supposed beforehand. A presupposition needs no basis in fact and no existing evidence. A presupposition involves expectation and a sort of dynamic tension that pulls you toward its object.

If someone presupposes they are a loser, they will tend to dismiss any facts to the contrary. They might experience a number of successes in work, finances, and relationships, but they will discount these successes as not being "the real thing." Yet, let them experience even one failure and, bingo!, that proves what they thought all along: They are a loser. Presuppositions are very powerful and, for the most part, elusive. You often have to develop very good insight before you can begin to identify some of your own

---

This material was originally discussed in Lankton, S. & Lankton, C. (1983). *The Answer Within*, p. 331; and, Lankton & Lankton, (1989). *Tales of Enchantment*, p. 209.

powerful presuppositions. Each of us have many – some are beneficial and some are detrimental to our well-being and happiness.

Even more interesting is that most people have never figured out how to construct their own beneficial presuppositions. But you can easily use your conscious intention to do just that. When you construct powerful presuppositions they continue to influence your life and your interpretation of your activities without much, if any, conscious effort on your part. Furthermore, they will operate well into the future depending upon how you construct them using the Emanated Image protocol.

Emanated Image is a tool that allows people to use their intention to deliberately create an emotionally rich and positive presupposition of success. Clinical work and personal experience both prove the veracity and unconscious longevity of performing this exercise.

Method

The key to making this protocol work for you is having *experience*. That doesn't mean "having experience" in the way the term is used in an employment interview (e.g., "I have experience in sales"). It means having sight, sound, smell, thoughts, beliefs, feelings, and emotions – that is *experience*. But there is a prescribed manner in which you have to have your experience.

In brief, you will imagine being in your ideal future, feel it as intensely as possible, and "think back" to the steps you took to arrive there. This is symbolically pictured in Illustration 10.

Future Shaping: Emanated-Images 69

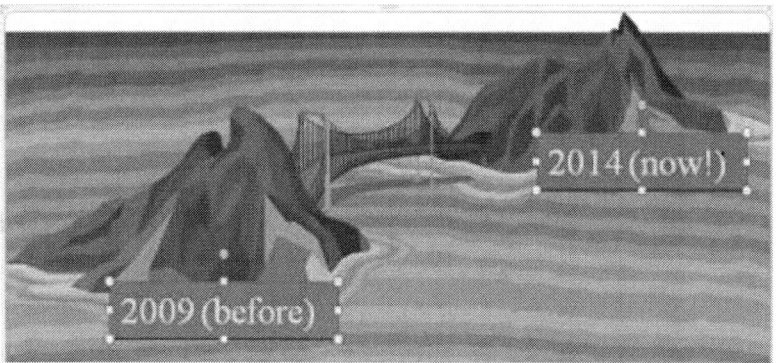

Illustration 10: Put yourself in the future, say 2014, and think back to the current date, say 2009. Consider the steps taken to get from there to where you are in the future.

Step 1: Become mindful of your breathing and relax or use a self-hypnosis method to prepare.

Step 2: Pick a time in the future when, if everything worked in your favor, you could have accomplished a desired set of goals. These goal could be employment, relationship, living arrangements, financial, personal, or so on. Let's say, for the sake of example, you think that in 5 years you would like to have a job you enjoy, a loving relationship, supportive friends, and be healthy. If it is 2009, you are going to imagine you are in the year 2014.

Step 3: In the state of heightened concentration begin to imagine you are in the future now. *Now, let me switch to speaking in present tense* – after all, we are now in a time that once was the future. To successfully have the imagination of the successful future you must begin to feel how satisfied and wonderful it is to have accomplished the job, found the relationship, and the friends and so on. This is absolutely crucial – you must feel the feelings and experience the emotions that accompany the success you worked toward for all these past years. Feel the joy of your success and let it change your breathing, let it bring a smile to your face, and saturate and spread throughout your body. Let yourself know you have really achieved what you had set out to achieve; appreciate yourself; let this awareness melt away any remaining subtle tensions; weep with joy if that is how you feel; but, live the success. After (and only after) you are feeling the joy of your accomplishments, move to the next step.

Step 4: While continuing to feel the success and joy think back to the year from which you originally started. Stay in the future with the good feelings and examine at least 6 major incidents that brought you here. As you think back and recall the "past" ask some questions about it and visualize the answers: What were some of the sacrifices you made to get here? What things or people did you let go of? Whom or what did you embrace? What were some of the solid-steps you took? What were some false steps you took? What major risks did you take? Whose help did you enlist? What did you do alone?

Ask these questions of yourself one at a time and think through the answers, visualizing your "past" behavior in each case. Remember to hold the positive feelings constant and in the foreground of your experience as you think through and "remember" the answer to each question. This step will take several minutes and the more detail you provide, and the more concretely you keep the successful feelings, the better.

Step 5: Let your mind relax and go blank. Become mindful of your breathing and sitting on your chair in the present time. Put no further thought into what had been the future as you open your eyes and return to the room.

What happens next? The next thing you should do is go about your business. You have created a presupposition that will operate to give shape to your understanding of your future actions. When you repeatedly use this tool you strengthen its effect - a conditioned positive emotional reaction to the various actions imagined during the steps you took. All the struggles, risks, and gains you reviewed in step 4 will initiate positive feelings of success instead of whatever fears, worries, and anxieties they might have previously triggered.

Use this tool for both large and small goals and tasks and for distant future and relatively eminent events. There is no limit to how much you will learn from yourself in step 4 and how much this tool can prepare you to collect positive feelings as you work toward achieving them. Consider this tool as a compliment to Vivid

72 Future Shaping: Emanated-Images

Symbolic Imagery and Self-Image Thinking. When you do Vivid Symbolic Imagery you are using your intention to collect feelings from the past and making them a reality in the present. When you do Self-Image Thinking you are using your intention to take desirable feelings and experiences from the present and engineering their occurrence in the future. Finally, when you use Emanated Images you are using your intention to imagine positive experiences in the future and bringing those back to the present. In summary you are using your mind to stimulate experiences past to present, present to future, and future to present, respectively. Nothing like this set of tools exists anywhere else – and they are invaluable for those who practice them.

10. Self-Reparenting and Self-Nurturing Spirals

The manner in which people, as children, were treated by their caretakers, unless deliberately changed, is the manner in which they treat themselves throughout adulthood. (For the sake of this chapter "caretakers" will be referred to as parents" for simplicity.) Their interactions with others is usually the way they responded to their parents or, again, the way their parents treated them. It is true that most people make minor corrections in those patterns owing to their judgment of what was obviously egregious to them in childhood. And finally it should be noted that, when interactions are defined by certain social contexts like work, school, and entertainment, people may interact according to conduct that was learned later in life. At work and school and some public events the rules of the social context may constrain the behaviors that people display in private. But, subtract the constraints of employment, school, and a few other contexts, and the above rules will generally and usually apply – especially in situations when stress levels increase.

If people were in a family where their parents seemed to criticize or correct every little thing they did, their minds will have been trained to think, anticipate, and allow experiences in accordance with that environment. Left unexamined and untrained, their mind will do exactly the same thing long after they have left home. They will postpone or even avoid accepting support. They will withhold support from others. They will discipline children with criticism and micromanagement. In some cases it will be so severe they will avoid feeling and showing any normal human weakness at all costs. In every case the toll it takes will be both personal and interpersonal. Not only will they suffer (although they will often have learned not to notice they are suffering) but also their intimate relations will suffer. Usually their marital bonds will be weakened and their relationship with their children will either be superficial or domineering.

Not all families are like that example, of course, but it is a useful analogy. The point is, whatever the unique communication style was in the family will be internalized by that individual and will become the 'map' for future interactions. In each case some behaviors and emotions will have been ignored, disallowed, punished and altered. For some emotions the result is what we consider good socialization and mature citizenship in our culture. But for other emotions, behaviors, and perceptions, it is a personal disaster.

For instance, a young girl who runs to her mother with excitement and is repeatedly ignored by her slightly depressed mother will learn to stop showing her joy and excitement. She will substitute other feelings and behaviors (and even perceptions) like trying to please and being sullen and serious. Later in life, feelings of joy and excitement may barely be detected by her or anyone around her. An important concern is, what toll does it take on a person to suppress natural feelings of excitement and joy for most of their life? This example was about excitement and joy but other examples would include dynamics that result in the suppression of fear, exploration, getting close, sadness, anger, tenderness, and even paying attention to others at all. Every person makes a unique substitution instead of showing their natural experiences.

What is the toll for this lifelong suppression? This yields our world's rescuers and victims and persecutors – all playing roles with which they have come to personally identify in an effort to meet deeper needs that never see the light of day (and therefore, never get satisfied). Everybody experiences some of this dynamic for different emotions to varying degrees. Some are so severe they are undisputable (e.g., obsessive-compulsive behaviors, depression, domestic violence, anxiety attacks, and child abuse, to name a few). Other less severe substitutes pass for "normal" and constitute the bulk of everyday life we encounter (e.g., the know- it-alls, bullies, placaters, flirts, control freaks, martyrs, busy bodies, outsiders, workaholics, and so on). These individuals are people whom we label with non-clinical phrases but the root of their difficulties is quite similar.

The result of such a real or perceived childhood learning is amenable to change. That is because a major part of what was learned was establishing habits of using bad chunking logic (as described in a previous chapter). People who have lived their lives in concert with previously critical/neglectful parent-child relations usually have come to think their negative interpretation of themselves and events is objective fact. They think it is correct to think they did a job that fell short of a necessary standard.

A crucial part of personal change is turning around such pervasive bad habits and even making the changes automatic and subconscious (just like the current bad habit). When first practicing this tool you may experience immediate but short term moments of clarity or relief. But, they are likely to fade rapidly – even within a matter of a few minutes. Why would that be? The answer lies in the fact that you have experienced years of learning and years of practicing negative self-nurturing. You have spent countless minutes over several years motivating yourself by means of disappointment and criticism. You have collected an astronomical number of negative experiences and you have postponed having many positive feelings almost indefinitely. And, you've kept it up automatically and subconsciously. It will take more than a few minutes of practice to change years of reinforced bad habits! To effectively make this change you *must* practice this tool repeatedly (and creative variants you may discover) on a daily basis. You should consider this the beginning of a new hobby aimed at reprogramming your mental habits.

It might be helpful to first recognize the extent of the negative self-comments that you make (especially if they are out of awareness). To best identify the out-of-awareness comment you might be making the following exercise is offered. Remember, this is only an exercise to create a heightened awareness of your situation.

Exercise to identify negative self talk.
1. Sit comfortably and develop relaxation or begin with a self-hypnosis exercise. Then retrieve a positive experience using any previous tool. Close your eyes

Self-Reparenting and Self-Nurturing Spirals 77

and visualize yourself in front of you about 3 feet away.

2. Imagining and seeing this projected self, do three things in the following order:

a. Say supportive, loving, kind, and accepting self-statements (if you need help, see the following list of self-nurturing comments).

b. Make critical, negative self-statements to the projected self (while you continue to feel comfortable with the earlier feeling). Continue making these negative comments for a couple of minutes.

c. Keeping the image of yourself in mind, again say supportive, loving, kind, and accepting self-statements as you did in sub-step "a." These must also continue for at least one minute or more.

Having now witnessed the ease of making a list of negative comments (compared to the ease of making a list of positive comments) you may be in a better position to appreciate how your inner dialog is more negative than positive. These negative methods of motivation are not healthy or enjoyable and they reduce creativity, productivity, health, and intimate relationships.

Simple Self-Nurturing Comments

It is often said that making self-nurturing comments is simply patting yourself on the back (Illustration 11). Ironically, that phrase, patting yourself on the back, is made into a derogatory concept. Maybe you have heard the comments like, "You are just

78 Self-Reparenting and Self-Nurturing Spirals

patting yourself on the back" used in the context to mean "don't be proud of yourself" or "don't brag." Kids who hear this sort of comment are even more unlikely to entertain the need for comforting and loving comments from a parent. This sort of condemnation is only another injustice done to the appropriate development of what otherwise might be a normal child. I'm going to weigh in on the side of supporting a person patting themselves on their back! As the father of three fantastic high-achieving children, I have anecdotal proof that this philosophy does not have detrimental results on children.

Sometimes I encounter people who have heard so few positive parent-child comments that they just don't know what to say in order to state one.

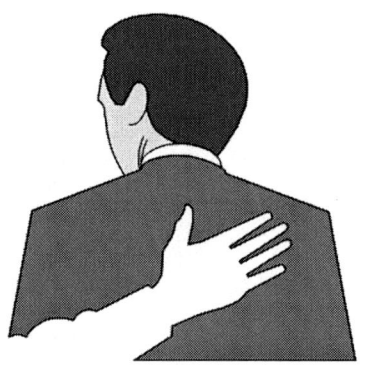

Illustration 11: Self-Nurturing

The following list should be of help getting you on the right path. Remember, each person will actually need different comments at different moments. It is necessary to monitor your mood and true feelings to create the most appropriate self-nurturing comments.

I'm proud of you
You're a great kid
You do wonderful things
You work so hard
It's okay to have your feelings
You're smart
I understand
You can do it
You've learned a lot
I love you
I'll be right here for you
I won't leave you
I'll help
Do what you can
You're handsome/beautiful
I like you
You're fun to be with

Self-Nurturing Spiral

The self-nurturing spiral protocol develops a state of mind free of negative self-talk, self-deprecatory comments, and judgmental comments. In addition, the goal is to learn to make supportive comments that reduce stress, eliminate depression, and build satisfaction and happiness. Regular daily use of the protocol will eventually condition experiences and self-talk to occur automatically and virtually replace your original habits of critical/neglectful parent-child comments and expectations. At that point a true self-reparenting will have become established based on your mature and thoughtful intentions.

Self-Nurturing Spiral Exercise

Step 1: List several supportive, accepting, and self-nurturing comments.

Step 2: Sit comfortably and become mindful of your breathing or use the self-hypnosis exercise.

Step 3: Imagine two figures behind you and place one on your left side and one on your right side.

Step 4: Imagine the figures taking turns speaking the comments from step one. As you imagine them speaking be sure to adjust the volume and tone of their speaking so that it is pleasant and confident. Do this for a duration of 3 or 4 breaths. Be sure to allow the voices to complete the entire sentences of your original comments. If at any time you can add new nurturing comments to the set of sentences, do so.

Step 5: Rotate the location of the voices so they seem to come from in front and behind you.

Step 6: Rotate the location of the voices again so they seem to have replaced each other on your right and left sides.

Step 7: Rotate the location of the voices again so they are at their original location.

Step 8: Rotate the two voices completely in a circle as you hear them speak again. Have the voices rotate around your ears as if they are coming from all directions (360 degrees) around you. Continue this encircling sound for several breaths.

Step 9: Raise this rotation to a foot-and-a-half above your head. Let the voices continue to rotate in a circle around you.

Step 10: Now bring the encircling sound back to the level of your ears, then lower it to your shoulders, then your chest, then your waist, your knees, your ankles, and finally your feet. At each stopping point allow the voices to make one complete rotation before moving them to the next stopping point.

Step 11: Bring the voices back up past each previous stop. And this time imagine them remaining at each location as you raise them to the next. That is, begin with a rotation at your feet and let that continue as you raise them to your ankles. Let them seem to remain at your feet and ankles as you raise them to your knees. Again, let them remain at your feet, ankles, and knees as you imagine them also present and encircling your waist. Continue this process until the voices are at every level (feet, ankles, knees, waist, chest, shoulders, ears, and above your head simultaneously). At this point they will be encircling you like a tube or a spiral and the supportive, accepting, and self-nurturing comments will be coming from every direction around you at all levels.

Step 12: Continue this self-nurturing spiral for six to ten slow breaths. Let your positive response fill your awareness. Let it saturate your experience as deeply as possible.

Step 13: Finally, imagine that the spiral of comments rises up far beyond your head and into the sky until it spirals out of sight. Let the bottom rise with it so you are left with the emotional response but the spiral is high above you.

11. Bioenergy and Chakra Balancing

This chapter concerns a method for developing a bodily awareness. Our physical body constitutes the largest part of our subconscious and unconscious. Yet most people live the majority of their life out of touch with their body. Your body constitutes the major portion of your feelings so you could say that most people, being out of touch with their body, are out of touch with their feelings. This is not to say that they are simply out of touch with their *emotions* - which they probably are – but that they are out of touch with their *feelings* when they ignore their body sensations. Communicating with others when you are out of touch with your feelings makes you superficial, cerebral, or controlling.

Before outlining the exercise I want to comment about the ancient chakra system. To begin, I need to say that there is no empirical research and no direct scientific evidence of the Hindu notion of a chakra system within the body. Yet, since I am going to direct you to concentrate on locations along your torso it would be an oversight to ignore this existing map of the chakras. For those who are entirely unfamiliar with this concept, the body chakras are said to be seven energy centers (Illustration 12). These correspond to the base of the spine (#1), the area just below the naval (#2), the solar plexus (#3), the heart (#4), the throat (#5), the area between and above the eyes (#6), and the crown of the head (#7). As it turns out, these so called energy centers of Eastern philosophy roughly

84 Bioenergy and Chakra Balancing

correspond to sympathetic ganglia identified in Western medicine as the sacro and hypogastric plexus and the parasympathetic ganglia know as the solar, cardio, and pharyngeal plexus. The third eye or pineal gland corresponds to the 6th chakra and the crown chakra corresponds to the soft area at the crown of the skull.

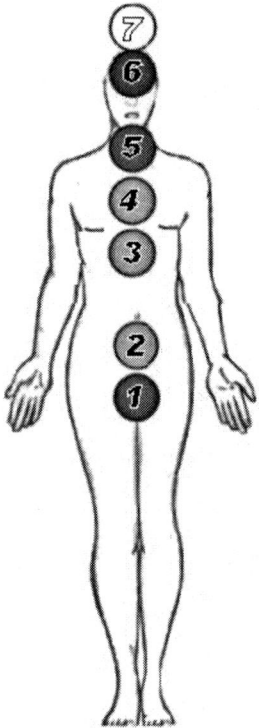

Illustration 12: The standard chakra locations

Illustration 12 shows the general placement of the standard system of seven chakras on the body. For this exercise we are primarily concerned with the locations identified as #2 through #6.

When one considers that these areas were identified by introspection (instead of dissection!) of the body it is most impressive. However, this exercise does not place a special premium on the chakras as sites of special subtle energy, per se. These areas for the balancing exercise were also chosen because they create a discrete array of locations throughout the body.

The concept of bioenergy has been in the field of psychology since an early understanding of it was introduced by Wilhelm Reich[2] in the 1930's. It has been continued and improved upon by many others over the years and the best known current proponent is Dr. Alexander Lowen, M.D.[3] Yet, the origins of the notion that energy flows throughout the body can be traced back to the Chinese system of medicine that employs the use of the body's meridian lines. Only scant empirical research has been directed on the existence of these lines. At Stanford University, William Tiller, Ph.D.[4] has reported detecting different electrical resistances comparing meridian lines to non-meridian areas of the skin. In any event, this exercise plays upon the notion that energy flow along the body can be stimulated.

The purpose of this exercise from a psychological point of view is to put you in touch with your body as a whole unit of wisdom. It is designed to unite your head with your body. Of, if you would like to put it this way, it is designed to get you in touch with your feelings. Note that this is "in touch with your feelings" and not "in touch with your emotions." Your feelings are created by the visceral information from your body. Most people, those who at any given moment are victims, rescuers, or persecutors, are out of touch with their feelings.

---

[2] Reich, W. (1945). *Character Analysis, 3nd Edition*. Simon and Schuster.
[3] Lowen, A. (1975). *Bioenergetics*. New York: Coward, McCann, & Geoghegan, Inc.
[4] Tillern, W. (1997). *Science and Human Transformation*. Pavior Publishing.

Chakra Energy Balancing Exercise

Step 1: Begin with a comfortable sitting posture and become mindful of your breathing or use one of the self-hypnosis exercises.

Step 2: Focus your attention on your palms and the soles of your feet and allow your awareness of them to heighten. After three or four breaths imagine or pretend that you are receiving energy from these contact points - energy from the Earth coming via the soles of your feet and energy from the air or sky via your palms. Allow this concept to develop for four to six more breaths.

Step 3: Next, imagine that the energy from your palms and soles is moving up through your arms and legs. Pretend your arms and legs are the conduits for energy to travel to your torso. Continue enriching this imagination for four to six more breaths.

Step 4: Imagine that there are four locations in your torso emitting energy from the intake of your hands and feet: your abdominal, solar plexus, heart, and throat chakra areas. Imagine that the energy emerges as if through a megaphone from those areas. If possible, imagine the energy is transmitted from these chakras both in front of you and behind you.

Step 5: Allow this imagination to continue to develop and be enriched for several breaths.

Step 6: If possible add the "third eye" chakra to the original four areas.

Step 7: Continue this imagination (energy entering your palms and soles and traveling up you arms and legs to finally be emerging from your 2st through 6th chakra) for several minutes.

Step 8: While this imagination continues you can use self-image thinking to make this total body awareness available in any future situations.

I encourage you to become proficient at this tool so you can quickly and easily use it from time to time throughout each day. It grounds you in an awareness of your body and enhances and enriches the impact you make on others. When you speak to them from such a grounded perspective your sincerity and intention will be conveyed and you will increase the likelihood of making your desired impression.

As for the empirical validly of any parts of this exercise, I have no convincing data. Reflexology is said to be 5,000 years old and originated in China. It possibly came from the work of the Taoists. Others have reported it originating with the practice of the Incas and predating China. Regarding the hands and feet, it suggests that the palms and the heels are points of energy contact that can supposedly stimulate various body organs. Imagining them as sources of energy contact is not meant to validate these assumption in anyway. It is simply a pretense wherein imagination builds on this ancient "wisdom" for a particular purpose. Indeed, that pretense and illusion may be all there has ever been to this so called wisdom. When you do the exercise you will gain a feeling of grounding and bodily awareness that is truly unique and useful to your intentions. It does not make the background material true. It means, instead, that this is a useful framework for achieving this desired outcome. It has been that way for centuries, actually! As with all of these exercises – indeed all of contemporary science – it is not about the truth of the theory but rather how useful it is for our purposes.

12. Responsibility and Empowerment

The tools of intention articulated in this book are a way in which you can use your conscious awareness to develop your mind, body, and relationships. Each tool was presented as a set of steps you can practice or teach to your clients, students, or children. I sometimes referred to them as protocols in this writing. In each protocol you are deliberately attempting to retrieve experiences. Because you are directing conscious attention I want to suggest a final step for each of these protocols. After doing an exercise and completing the steps of the protocol purposely put it out of your mind. That might seem odd unless your realize this: Your conscious intention is useful – but it is not completely correct and accurate. In many ways it does not accurately match reality. Our understanding of reality is always an approximation. So the last step is to put the entire exercise out of your mind and let your unconscious do the rest for you without your control. Doing the exercises gets your unconscious operating in the right direction. Then you need to relinquish control and let the rest happen according to a better understanding of your overall life – a function of your unconscious.

Responsibility

As psychotherapists we want every one of our clients to be able to take responsibility for their lives and the changes they seek. All too often we grasp for the tools to give them and the way to articulate the things they might do. Some of the most discouraging things we hear come from people who want us to "make their spouse trustworthy again," "make my child do well in school," "use hypnosis to make me stop over-eating," " cure my depression," "tell me what to do so I won't have panic attacks," "fix my marriage," "help my son who has bi-polar disorder." And the list can go on for pages. What everyone of these requests have in common is a loud message that says, "I am a passive person in the disorder/disease and I am a passive recipient of what therapy will give me or do to me."

Empowerment

The term "empowerment" means to make people able to take charge of their life. It is a term that has slipped out of use in the last decade. It seems that everywhere we turn we are told that we cannot handle our own lives. Apparently we can't handle our pain, eating, attention, sexual energies, sleeping, anxiety, moods, or practically anything according to the dominant cultural norm. Just turn on a television for a few hours and you will see that we are hopeless victims of various maladies - which have apparently come upon us through no action of our own - and which can be cured with an easily available drug. I may not be well liked by the pharmaceutical companies because I am not a supporter of anything less than asking, "How can I solve this problem that I, to some degree, created?"

I want to share two personal anecdotes to illustrate this. The first occurred when I was in high school. Both of my thighs and feet suffered 3rd degree burns from concentrated nitric acid in a chemistry lab accident. The skin on my thighs was burned away in patches as large as five by nine inches. The skin on the tops of both feet was totally gone. I used Teflon bandages and mustard cream of some sort and went to see a doctor every week or two. Finally, my doctor announced that I would need skin grafts because the skin would not grow. He knew this because the hair was not growing back. I didn't cherish the idea of having more places on my body to heal! I asked him how we could make the skin grow. He said that unless the hair follicles grew the skin would not come back. I asked how we can make the hair grow. He said, "If I know that I would become rich helping every bald man in the world!" Again I inquired what I might do to help the hair grow and he said the following. He told me to read about and view pictures on how hair cells grow. Then at night while I soak my legs and feet I should imagine the cells growing. He said I should visualize hair growing like weeds in a field or grass in a lawn. I remember asking if that would work and he replied, "It won't hurt - it *has* helped some people." So that was exactly what I did.

When I returned for my next visit a few weeks later, he was ecstatic. It said the hair was growing...the skin would grow...I had succeeded to overcome the odds and make my body regenerate. I was 16 years old.

The next anecdote I want to share took place when I was 40 years old. My dental hygienist in Florida said that I would need periodontal surgery because there was a "pocket" 8.25 mm deep on the side of my upper-left wisdom tooth. I told her I would fix it. She misunderstood and thought I meant that I would see a surgeon. She said in surprise that she never talked anyone into that so easily. But I clarified that I would fix it. She replied that I would have to grow tissue to do that. I said, "OK." She said, "You can't do that - you would have to grow bone. You can't grow bone." I raised my arms and said, "Well, how do you think I got these?!" About that time my dentist, Randal Bailey, came in the room. She appealed to him for support. But, Dr. Bailey had dealt with me for years and replied, "Well, you've got to make a little room for Steve - he's different." When I returned 4 months later for the next checkup that pocket was 3.25 mm. But everyone knows, "You can't grow bone" - right?

My personal story of success includes examples of removing pains, back injuries, social and psychological gains and more. And the gains of my clients, over the years, make the list of self-improvements too long to relate in this book. But, the point of these two anecdotes and others like it is to show examples of being empowered. You see, despite the hygienist, I remained confident about my ability to make my body heal. Of course, that confidence was built on my teenage experience of hair and skin growth and many other successes after that. The question I leave you with is, "How much *can* we do to cure ourselves?" Because contemporary culture seems to imply that we can't do anything to help ourselves at all.

It is not my goal to make readers turn away from whatever treatment they are receiving. Actually, most people would probably fail to replicate my results in every one of these areas. That is because most people have years of history of interactions successfully convincing them that they are incapable of making change without drugs or surgery or reliance upon others. For those people, that is absolutely true - currently.

Yet, I can't help but know that if I can be empowered to make changes that some consider dramatic, then most everyone can.

We have to begin somewhere – and we have to begin now. The only way we will change this trend and come to embrace our power and capability is to begin empowering ourselves. If you have social anxiety you need to learn to retrieve experiences of calm and confidence with vivid symbolic imagery and associate them to social interactions with self-image thinking. If you are depressed you need to be especially mindful of chunking logic and then do the same with every positive experience as often as possible. If you have erectile dysfunction, panic, attention problems, over-eating, insecurity, obsession, and any of a myriad of social or psychological problems you are not being empowered. You do not know how to express your intention for your own betterment.

Our parents, schools, employers, and friends have all grown up within this dis-empowering culture. There aren't many places one can turn to learn the opposite. Ironically, our culture purports to be a champion of happiness and self-management. Our Declaration of Independence "hold it to self-evident." Judeo-Christian religions permit it. Most of our parents wish it. Indeed, it often appears that our institutions can only give lip-service to the claims that we may/can/should be happy and in control. I'm not sure that happy and satisfied people make good consumers so I doubt that Madison Avenue – the media- really wants us happy and in control of our lives. As a result, most people never come upon the tools to accomplish gaining a feeling of happiness and control..

Many *many* psychotherapists want nothing more than to help their clients find methods that will empower them and make it possible for them to take change into their own hands. Still, there are too few books and seminars that really spell out the simple mechanics of what a person can do. Learning to be happy and healthy and learning the tools to maintain it constitutes nothing less than a small social revolution for each person who succeeds.

My hope is that this book is one of the best compilations of tools you have seen. The bottom line of all this material is that you have to get the resources that are needed in each situation in your life. *That's* the secret. Knowing what those resources are is a big help, of course. Having the tools to build them and get them is what this book is all about. The most beneficial use of this material will occur when you grasp the principles and methods written in each exercise and make them your own. This might involve practicing each tool until you realize what is as the heart of it and then modifying it and then using it so it fits your life. I hope you begin immediately.

Authored books by Stephen R. Lankton

Lankton, S., & Lankton, C. (2008). *The answer within: A clinical framework of Ericksonian hypnotherapy.* This book was originally published in 1983 by Brunner Mazel Publishers and is now published in paperback by Crown House Publishing, Bethel, CT.

Lankton, S., & Lankton, C. (2007). *Enchantment and intervention in family therapy: Using metaphors in family therapy.* This book was originally published in 1986 by Brunner Mazel Publishers and is now published in paperback by Crown House Publishing, Bethel, CT.

Lankton, S. (2004). *Assembling Ericksonian therapy: The collected papers of Stephen Lankton.* Phoenix: Zeig,Tucker, and Theisen Publishers.

Lankton, S. (2003). *Practical magic: A translation of basic neuro linguistic programming into clinical psychotherapy* (Rev. ed.). This book was originally published in 1980 by Meta Publications and is now published in paperback by Crown House Publishing, Bethel, CT.

Lankton, C., & Lankton, S. (1989). *Tales of enchantment: Goal Directed Metaphors for Adults and Children in Therapy.* New York: Brunner Mazel.

Lankton, S. (1988). *A children's book to overcome Fears: The blammo - surprise book!.* New York: Brunner Mazel.

Edited books by Stephen R. Lankton

Lankton, S., & Zeig, J. (Eds.). (1994). *Ericksonian monographs: Number 10. Difficult Contexts for Therapy.* New York: Brunner Mazel.

Lankton, S., & Erickson, K. (Eds.). (1993). *Ericksonian monographs: Number 9. Essence of single session success.* New York: Brunner Mazel.

Lankton, S., Gilligan, S., & Zeig, J. (Eds.). (1991). *Views on Ericksonian brief therapy, process and action: Number 8.* New York: Brunner Mazel.

Lankton, S. (Ed.). (1990). *Ericksonian monographs: Number 7. Broader implications of Ericksonian therapy.* New York: Brunner Mazel.

Lankton, S., & Zeig, J. (Eds.). (1989). *Ericksonian monographs: Number 6. Extrapolations: Demonstrations of Ericksonian therapy.* New York: Brunner Mazel.

Lankton, S. (Ed.). (1989). *Ericksonian monographs: Number 5. Ericksonian hypnosis: Application, preparation, and research.* New York: Brunner Mazel.

Zeig, J., & Lankton, S. (Eds.). (1988). *Developing Ericksonian psychotherapy: State of the arts. The proceedings of the third international congress on Ericksonian psychotherapy.* New York: Brunner Mazel.

Lankton, S., & Zeig, J. (Eds.). (1988). *Ericksonian monographs: Number 4. Research comparisons and medical applications.* New York: Brunner Mazel.

Lankton, S., & Zeig, J. (Eds.). (1988). *Ericksonian monographs: Number 3. Special treatment populations.* New York: Brunner Mazel.

Lankton, S. (Ed.). (1987). *Ericksonian monographs: Number 2. Central themes and underlying principles.* New York: Brunner Mazel.

Lankton, S. (Ed.). (1985). *Ericksonian monographs: Number 1. Elements and dimensions of an Ericksonian approach.* New York: Brunner Mazel.

About the Author

Stephen R. Lankton, MSW, DAHB, is a licensed Clinical Social Worker in Phoenix, Arizona. He is Editor of the *American Journal of Clinical Hypnosis*, and executive director of the Phoenix Institute of Ericksonian Therapy. He is an appointed member of the Arizona Behavioral Health Examiners Board, Credentialing Committee. He is a Diplomate in Clinical Hypnosis, and past-president of the American Hypnosis Board for Clinical Social Work. He is a Fellow of the American Society of Clinical Hypnosis; a Fellow of the American Association of Marriage and Family Therapy; and a Fellow of the American Psychotherapy Association. He is a recipient of the Milton H. Erickson Foundation "Lifetime Achievement Award" for outstanding contributions to the field of psychotherapy, and of the ASCH "Irving Secter Award" for the advancement of clinical hypnosis. He is author of 18 clinical books with translations in several languages regarding techniques of hypnosis, family therapy, and brief therapy. He has a clinical practice in Phoenix and trains health care professionals internationally.